Platform Thirteen is different.

Spiders have spun their webs across the cloakroom door. There's a Left-Luggage Office with a notice saying NOT IN USE. The chocolate machines are rusty and lopsided, and if you were foolish enough to put your money in one, it would make a noise like "Harrumph" and swallow it.

Yet when people tried to pull down that part of the station and redevelop it, something always went wrong. An architect who wanted to build shops there suddenly came out in awful boils and went to live in Spain, and when they tried to relay the tracks for electricity, the surveyor said the ground wasn't suitable. It was as though people knew something about Platform Thirteen, but they didn't know what.

The Secret of
PLATFORM 13

• • • • • • • • • • •

Eva Ibbotson

Illustrated by Sue Porter

SCHOLASTIC INC.
New York Toronto London Auckland Sydney
Mexico City New Delhi Hong Kong

ISBN 0-439-26768-4

12 11 10 9 8 7 6 5 4 3 2   0 1 2 3 4 5/0

Printed in the U.S.A.   40

First Scholastic printing, December 2000

For Laurie and for David

THE SECRET OF
PLATFORM 13

CHAPTER 1

IF YOU WENT into a school nowadays and said to the children: "What is a *gump*?" you would probably get some very silly answers.

"It's a person without a brain, like a chump," a child might say. Or:

"It's a camel whose hump has got stuck." Or even:

"It's a kind of chewing gum."

But once this wasn't so. Once every child in the land could have told you that a gump was a special mound, a grassy bump on the earth, and that in this bump was a hidden door which opened every so often to reveal a tunnel which led to a completely different world.

They would have known that every country has its own gump and that in Great Britain the gump was in a place called the Hill of the Cross of Kings not far from the river Thames. And the wise children, the ones that read the old stories and listened to the old tales, would have known more than that. They would have known that this particular gump opened for exactly nine days every nine years, and not one second longer, and that it was no good changing your mind about coming or going because nothing would open the door once the time was up.

But the children forgot—everyone forgot—and perhaps you can't blame them, yet the gump is still there. It is under Platform Thirteen of King's Cross Railway Station, and the secret door is behind the wall of the old gentlemen's cloakroom with its flappy posters saying "Trains Get You There" and its chipped wooden benches and the dirty ashtrays in which the old gentlemen used to stub out their smelly cigarettes.

No one uses the platform now. They have built newer, smarter platforms with rows of shiny luggage trolleys and slot machines that actually work and television screens which show you how late your train is going to be. But Platform Thirteen is different. The clock has stopped; spiders have spun their webs across the cloakroom door. There's a Left-Luggage Office with a notice saying NOT IN USE, and inside it is an umbrella covered in mold which a lady left on the 5:25 from Doncaster the year of the Queen's Silver Jubilee. The chocolate machines are rusty and lopsided, and if you were foolish enough to put your money in one, it would make a noise like "Harrumph" and swallow it, and you could wait the rest of your life for the chocolate to come out.

Yet when people tried to pull down that part of the station and redevelop it, something always went wrong. An architect who wanted to build shops there suddenly came out in awful boils and went to live in Spain, and when they tried to relay the tracks for electricity, the surveyor said the ground wasn't suitable and muttered something about subsidence and cracks. It was as though people knew *something* about Platform Thirteen, but they didn't know what.

But in every city there are those who have not forgotten the old days or the old stories. The ghosts, for example . . . Ernie Hobbs, the railway porter who'd spent all his life working at King's Cross and still liked to haunt round the trains, he knew—and so did his friend, the ghost of a cleaning lady called Mrs. Partridge who used to scrub out the parcels' office on her hands and knees. The people who plodged about in the sewers under the city and came up occasionally through the manholes beside the station, they knew . . . and so in their own way did the pigeons.

They knew that the gump was still there and they knew where it led: by a long, misty, and mysterious tunnel to a secret cove where a ship waited to take those who wished it to an island so beautiful that it took the breath away.

The people who lived on it just called it the Island, but it has had all sorts of names: Avalon, St. Martin's Land, the Place of the Sudden Mists. Years and years ago it was joined to the mainland, but then it broke off and floated away slowly westward, just as Madagascar floated away from the continent of Africa. Islands do that every few million years; it is nothing to make a fuss about.

With the floating island, of course, came the people who were living on it: sensible people mostly who understood that everyone did not have to have exactly two arms and legs, but might be different in shape and different in the way they thought. So they lived peacefully with ogres who had one eye or dragons (of whom there were a lot about in those days). They didn't leap into the sea every time they saw a mermaid comb her hair on a rock. They simply said, "Good morning." They understood that Ellerwomen had hollow backs and hated to be looked at on a Saturday and that if trolls wanted to wear their beards so long that they stepped on them every time they walked, then that was entirely their own affair.

They lived in peace with the animals too. There were

a lot of interesting animals on the Island as well as ordinary sheep and cows and goats. Giant birds who had forgotten how to fly and laid eggs the size of kettle drums, and brollachans like blobs of jelly with dark red eyes, and sea horses with manes of silk that galloped and snorted in the waves.

But it was the mistmakers that the people of the Island loved the most. These endearing animals are found nowhere else in the world. They are white and small with soft fur all over their bodies, rather like baby seals, but they don't have flippers. They have short legs and big feet like the feet of puppies. Their black eyes are huge and moist, their noses are whiskery and cool, and they pant a little as they move because they look rather like small pillows and they don't like going very fast.

The mistmakers weren't just *nice*, they were exceedingly important.

Because as the years passed and newspapers were washed up on the shore or refugees came through the gump with stories of the World Above, the Islanders became more and more determined to be left alone. Of course they knew that some modern inventions were good, like electric blankets to keep people's feet warm in bed or fluoride to stop their teeth from rotting, but there were other things they didn't like at all, like nuclear weapons or tower blocks at the tops of which old ladies shivered and shook because the lifts were bust, or battery hens stuffed two in a cage. And they dreaded being discovered by passing ships or airplanes flying too low.

Which is where the mistmakers came in. These sensitive creatures, you see, absolutely adore music. When you play music to a mistmaker, its eyes grow wide and it lets out its breath and gives a great sigh.

"Aaah," it will sigh. "Aaah . . . aaah . . ."

And each time it sighs, mist comes from its mouth: clean, thick, white mist which smells of early morning and damp grass. There are hundreds and hundreds of mistmakers lolloping over the turf or along the shore of the Island, and that means a lot of mist.

So when a ship was sighted or a speck in the sky which might be an airplane, all the children ran out of school with their flutes and their trumpets and their recorders and started to play to the mistmakers . . . And the people who might have landed and poked and pried saw only clouds of whiteness and went on their way.

Though there were so many unusual creatures on the Island, the royal family was entirely human and always had been. They were royal in the proper sense—not greedy, not covered in jewels, but brave and fair. They saw themselves as servants of the people, which is how all good rulers should think of themselves, but often don't.

The King and Queen didn't live in a golden palace full of uncomfortable gilded thrones which stuck into people's behinds when they sat down, nor did they fill the place with servants who fell over footstools from walking backward from Their Majesties. They lived in a low white house on a curving beach of golden sand studded with cowrie shells—and always, day or night, they could hear the murmur and slap of the waves and the gentle soughing of the wind.

The rooms of the palace were simple and cool; the windows were kept open so that birds could fly in and out. Intelligent dogs lay sleeping by the hearth; bowls of fresh fruit and fragrant flowers stood on the tables—and anyone who had nowhere to go—orphaned little hags or seals with sore flippers or wizards who had become depressed and old—found sanctuary there.

And in the year 1983—the year the Americans put a woman into space—the Queen, who was young and kind and beautiful—had a baby. Which is where this story really begins.

The baby was a boy, and it was everything a baby should be, with bright eyes, a funny tuft of hair, a button nose, and interesting ears. Not only that, but the little Prince could whistle before he was a month old—not proper tunes, but a nice peeping noise like a young bird.

The Queen was absolutely besotted about her son, and the King was so happy that he thought he would burst, and all over the Island the people rejoiced because you can tell very early how a baby is going to turn out, and they could see that the Prince was going to be just the kind of ruler that they wanted.

Of course as soon as the child was born, there were queues of people round the palace wanting to look after him and be his nurse: Wise Women who wanted to teach him things and sirens who wanted to sing to him and hags who wanted to show him weird tricks. There was even a mermaid who seemed to think she could look after a baby, even if it meant she had to be trundled round the palace in a bath on wheels.

But although the Queen thanked everyone most politely, the nurse she chose for her baby was an ordinary human. Or rather it was three ordinary humans: triplets whose names were Violet and Lily and Rose. They had come to the Island as young girls and were proper trained nursery nurses who knew how to change nappies and bring up wind and sieve vegetables, and the fact that they couldn't do any magic was a relief to the Queen who sometimes felt she had enough magic in her life. Having triplets seemed to her a good idea because looking after babies goes on night and day, and this way there would always be someone with spiky red hair and a long nose and freckles to soothe the Prince and rock him and sing to him, and he wouldn't be startled by the change because however remarkable the baby was, he wouldn't be able to tell Violet from Lily or Lily from Rose.

So the three nurses came and they did indeed look after the Prince most devotedly and everything went beautifully—for a while. But when the baby was three months old, there came the time of the Opening of the Gump—and after that, nothing was ever the same again.

There was always excitement before the Opening. In the harbor, the sailors made the three-masted ship ready to sail to the Secret Cove; those people who wanted to leave the Island started their packing and said their good-byes, and rest houses were prepared for those who would come the other way.

It was now that homesickness began to attack Lily and Violet and Rose.

Homesickness is a terrible thing. Children at boarding schools sometimes feel as though they're going to die of it. It doesn't matter what your home is like—it's that it's yours that matters. Lily and Violet and Rose loved the Island and they adored the Prince, but now they began to remember the life they had led as little girls in the shabby streets of north London.

"Do you remember the Bingo Halls?" asked Lily. "All the shouting from inside when someone won?"

"And Saturday night at the Odeon with a bag of crisps?" said Violet.

"The clang of the fruit machines in Paddy's Parlour," said Rose.

They went on like this for days, quite forgetting how unhappy they had been as children: teased at school, never seeing a clean blade of grass, and beaten by their father. So unhappy that they'd taken to playing in King's Cross Station and had been there when the door opened in the gump and couldn't go through it fast enough.

"I know we can't go Up There," said Lily. "Not with the Prince to look after. But maybe Their Majesties would let us sail with the ship and just look at the dear old country?"

So they asked the Queen if they could take the baby Prince on the ship and wait with him in the Secret Cove—and the Queen said no. The thought of being parted from her baby made her stomach crunch up so badly that she felt quite sick.

It was because she minded so much that she began to change her mind. Was she being one of those awful drooling mothers who smother children instead of letting them grow up free and unafraid? She spoke to the King, hoping he would forbid his son to go, but he said: "Well, dear, it's true that adventures are good for people even when they are very young. Adventures can get into a person's blood even if he doesn't remember having them. And surely you trust the nurses?"

Well, she did, of course. And she trusted the sailors who manned the ship—and sea air, as everybody knows, is terribly good for the lungs.

So she agreed and had a little weep in her room, and the nurses took the baby aboard in his handwoven rush basket with its lace-edged hood and settled him down for the voyage.

Just before the ship was due to sail, the Queen rushed out of the palace, her face as white as chalk, and said: "No, no! Bring him back! I don't want him to go!"

But when she reached the harbor, she was too late. The ship was just a speck in the distance, and only the gulls echoed her tragic voice.

CHAPTER 2

MRS. TROTTLE was rich. She was so rich that she had eleven winter coats and five diamond necklaces, and her bath had golden taps. Mr. Trottle, her husband, was a banker and spent his days lending money to people who already had too much of it and refusing to lend it to people who needed it. The house the Trottles lived in was in the best part of London beside a beautiful park and not far from Buckingham Palace. It had an ordinary address, but the tradesmen called it Trottle Towers because of the spiky railings that surrounded it and the statues in the garden and the flagpole.

Although Larina Trottle was perfectly strong and well and Landon Trottle kept fit by hiring a man to pummel him in his private gym, the Trottles had no less than five servants to wait on them: a butler, a cook, a chauffeur, a housemaid, and a gardener. They had three cars and seven portable telephones, which Mr. Trottle sat on sometimes by mistake, and a hunting lodge in Scotland where he went to shoot deer, and a beach house in the South of France with a flat roof on which Mrs. Trottle lay with nothing on, so as to get a suntan, which was *not* a pleasant sight.

But there was one thing they didn't have. They didn't have a baby.

As the years passed and no baby came along, Mrs. Trottle got angrier and angrier. She glared at people pushing prams, she snorted when babies appeared on television gurgling and advertising disposable nappies. Even puppies and kittens annoyed her.

Then after nearly ten years of marriage, she decided to go and adopt a baby.

First, though, she went to see the woman who had looked after her when she was small. Nanny Brown was getting on in years. She was a tiny, grumpy person who soaked her false teeth in brandy and never got into bed without looking to see if there was a burglar hiding underneath, but she knew everything there was to know about babies.

"You'd better come with me," Mrs. Trottle said. "And I want that old doll of mine."

So Nanny Brown went to fetch the doll, which was one of the large, old-fashioned ones with eyes that click open and shut, and lace dresses, and cold, china arms and legs.

And on a fine day toward the end of June, the chauffeur drove Mrs. Trottle to an orphanage in the north of England, and beside her in the Rolls-Royce sat Nanny Brown, looking like a cross old bird and holding the china doll in her lap.

They reached the orphanage. Mrs. Trottle swept in.

"I have come to choose a baby," she said. "I'm prepared to take either a boy or a girl, but it must be healthy, of course, and not more than three months old, and I'd prefer it to have fair hair."

Matron looked at her. "I'm afraid we don't have any babies for adoption," she said. "There's a waiting list."

"A *waiting list!*" Mrs. Trottle's bosom swelled so much that it looked as if it were going to take off into space. "My good woman, do you know who I am? I am Larina Trottle! My husband is the head of Trottle and Blatherspoon, the biggest merchant bank in the City, and his salary is five hundred thousand pounds a year."

Matron said she was glad to hear it.

"Anyone lucky enough to become a Trottle would be brought up like a prince," Mrs. Trottle went on. "And this doll which I have brought for the baby is a real antique. I have been offered a very large sum of money for it. This doll is priceless!"

Matron nodded and said she was sure Mrs. Trottle was right, but she had no babies for adoption, and that was her last word.

The journey back to London was not a pleasant one. Mrs. Trottle ranted and raved; Nanny Brown sat huddled up with the doll in her lap; the chauffeur drove steadily southward.

Then just as they were coming into London, the engine began to make a nasty clunking noise.

"Oh no, this is too much!" raged Mrs. Trottle. "I will *not* allow you to break down in these disgusting, squalid streets." They were close to King's Cross Station, and it was eleven o'clock at night.

But the clunking noise grew worse.

"I'm afraid I'll have to stop at this garage, Madam," said the chauffeur.

They drew up by one of the petrol pumps. The chauffeur got out to look for a mechanic.

Mrs. Trottle, in the backseat, went on ranting and raving.

Then she grew quiet. On a bench between the

garage and a fish-and-chip shop sat a woman whose frizzy red hair and long nose caught the lamplight. She was wearing the uniform of a nursery nurse and beside her was a baby's basket . . . a basket most finely woven out of rushes whose deep hood sheltered whoever lay within.

The chauffeur returned with a mechanic and began to rev the engine. Exhaust fumes from the huge car drifted toward the bench where the red-haired woman sat holding on to the handle of the basket. Her head nodded, but she jerked herself awake.

The chauffeur revved even harder, and another cloud of poisonous gas rolled toward the bench.

The nurse's head nodded once more.

"Give me the doll!" ordered Larina Trottle—and got out of the car.

For eight days the nurses had waited on the ship as it anchored off the Secret Cove. They had sung to the Prince and rocked him and held him up to see the sea birds and the cliffs of their homeland. They had taken him ashore while they paddled and gathered shells, and they had welcomed the people who came through the gump, as they arrived in the mouth of the cave.

Traveling through the gump takes only a moment. The suction currents and strange breezes that are stored up there during nine long years have their own laws and can form themselves into wind baskets into which people can step and be swooshed up or down in an instant. It is a delightful way to travel but can be muddling for those not used to it, and the nurses made themselves useful helping the newcomers onto the ship.

Then on the ninth day something different came through the tunnel . . . and that something was—a smell.

The nurses were right by the entrance in the cliff when it came to them and as they sniffed it up, their eyes filled with tears.

"Oh Lily!" said poor Violet, and her nose quivered.

"Oh Rose!" said poor Lily and clutched her sister.

It was the smell of their childhood: the smell of fish and chips. Every Saturday night their parents had sent them out for five packets, and they'd carried them back, warm as puppies, through the lamplit streets.

"Do you remember the batter, all sizzled and gold?" asked Lily.

"And the soft whiteness when you got through to the fish?" said Violet.

"The way the chips went soggy when you doused them with vinegar?" said Rose.

And as they stood there, they thought they would die if they didn't just once more taste the glory that was fish and chips.

"We can't go," said Lily, who was the careful one. "You know we can't."

"Why can't we?" asked Rose. "We'd be up there in a minute. It's a good two hours still before the Closing."

"What about the Prince? There's no way we can leave him," said Lily.

"No, of course we can't," said Violet. "We'll take him. He'll love going in a swoosherette, won't you, my poppet?"

And indeed the Prince crowed and smiled and looked as though he would like nothing better.

Well, to cut a long story short, the three sisters made their way to the mouth of the cave, climbed into a wind basket—and in no time at all found themselves in King's Cross Station.

Smells are odd things. They follow you about when you're not thinking about them, but when you put your nose to where they ought to be, they aren't there. The nurses wandered round the shabby streets, and to be honest they were wishing they hadn't come. The pavements were dirty, passing cars splattered them with mud, and the Odeon Cinema where they'd seen such lovely films had been turned into a bowling alley.

Then suddenly there it was again—the smell— stronger than ever, and now, beside an All Night garage, they saw a shop blazing with light and in the window a sign saying FRYING NOW.

The nurses hurried forward. Then they stopped.

"We can't take the Prince into a common fish-and-chip shop," said Lily. "It wouldn't be proper."

The others agreed. Some of the people queuing inside looked distinctly rough.

"Look, you wait over there on the bench with the baby," said Rose. She was half an hour older than the others and often took the lead. "Violet and I'll go in and get three packets. We're only a couple of streets away from the station—there's plenty of time."

So Lily went to sit on the bench, and Rose and Violet went in to join the queue. Of course when they reached the counter, the cod had run out—something always runs out when it's your turn. But the man went to fetch some more and there was nothing to worry about: they had three-quarters of an hour before the Closing of the Gump, and they were only ten minutes' walk from the station.

Lily, waiting on the bench, saw the big Rolls Royce draw up at the garage . . . saw the chauffeur get out and a woman with wobbly piled-up hair open the window and let out a stream of complaints.

Then the chauffeur came back and started to rev up . . .

Oh dear, I do feel funny, thought Lily, and held on tight to the handle of the basket. Her head fell forward and she jerked herself awake. Another cloud of fumes rolled toward her . . . and once more she blacked out.

But only for a moment. Almost at once she came round and all was well. The big car had gone, the basket was beside her, and now her sisters came out with three packets wrapped in newspaper. The smell was marvelous, and a greasy ooze had come up on the face of the Prime Minister, just the way she remembered it.

Thoroughly pleased with themselves, the nurses hurried through the dark streets, reached Platform Thirteen, and entered the cloakroom.

Only when they were safe in the tunnel did they unpack the steaming fish and chips.

"Let's just give him one chip to suck?" suggested Violet.

But Lily, who was the fussy one, said no, the Prince only had healthy food and never anything salty or fried.

"He's sleeping so soundly," she said fondly.

She bent over the cot, peered under the hood . . . unwound the embroidered blanket, the lacy shawl . . .

Then she began to scream.

Instead of the warm, living, breathing baby—there lay a cold and lifeless doll.

And the wall of the gentlemen's cloakroom was moving . . . moving . . . it was almost back in position.

Weeping, clawing, howling, the nurses tried to hold it back.

Too late. The gump was closed, and no power on earth could open it again before the time was up.

But in Nanny Brown's little flat, Mrs. Trottle stood looking down at the stolen baby with triumph in her eyes.

"Do you know what I'm going to do?" she said.

Nanny Brown shook her head.

"I'm going to go right away from here with the baby. To Switzerland. For a whole year. And when I come back I'm going to pretend that I had him over there. That it's my very own baby—not adopted but *mine*. No one will guess; it's such a little baby. My husband won't guess either if I stay away—he's so busy with the bank, he won't notice."

Nanny Brown looked at her, thunderstruck. "You'll never get away with it, Miss Larina. Never."

"Oh yes, I will! I'm going to bring him back as my own little darling babykins, aren't I, my poppet? I'm going to call him Raymond. Raymond Trottle, that sounds good, doesn't it? He's going to grow up like a little prince, and no one will be sorry for me or sneer at me because they'll think he's properly mine. I'll sack all the servants and get some new ones so they can't tell tales, and when I come back, it'll be with my teeny weeny Raymond in my arms."

"You can't do it," said Nanny Brown obstinately. "It's wicked."

"Oh yes, I can. And you're going to give up your flat and come with me because I'm not going to change his nappies. And if you don't, I'll go to the police and tell them it was you that stole the baby."

"You wouldn't!" gasped Nanny Brown.

But she knew perfectly well that Mrs. Trottle would. When she was a little girl, Larina Trottle had tipped five live goldfish onto the carpet and watched them flap themselves to death because her mother had told her to clean out their bowl, and she was capable of anything.

But it wasn't just fear that made Nanny Brown go with Mrs. Trottle to Switzerland. It was the baby with his milky breath and the big eyes which he now opened to look about him and the funny little whistling noise he made. She wasn't a particularly nice woman, but she loved babies, and she knew that Larina Trottle was as fit to look after a young baby as a baboon. Actually, a lot *less* fit because baboons, as it happens, make excellent mothers.

So Mrs. Trottle went away to Switzerland—and over the Island a kind of darkness fell. The Queen all but died of grief, the King went about his work like a man twice his age. The people mourned, the mermaids wept on their rocks, and the schoolchildren made a gigantic calendar showing the number of days which had to pass before the gump opened once more and the Prince could be brought back.

But of all this, the boy called Raymond Huntingdon Trottle knew nothing at all.

CHAPTER 3

ODGE GRIBBLE was a hag.

She was a very young one, and a disappointment to
her parents. The Gribbles lived in the north of the
Island and came from a long line of frightful and monstrous women who flapped and shrieked about, giving
nightmares to people who had been wicked or making
newts come out of the mouths of anyone who told a lie.
Odge's oldest sister had a fingernail so long that you
could dig the garden with it, the next girl had black

hairs like piano wires coming out of her ears, the third had stripey feet and so on—down to the sixth who had blue teeth and a wart the size of a saucer on her chin.

Then came Odge.

There was great excitement before she was born because Mrs. Gribble had herself been a seventh daughter, and now the new baby would be the seventh also, and the seventh daughter of a seventh daughter is supposed to be very special indeed.

But when the baby came, everyone fell silent and a cousin of Mrs. Gribble's said: "Oh dear!"

The baby's fingernails were short; not one whisker grew out of her ears; her feet were absolutely ordinary.

"She looks just like a small pink splodge," the cousin went on.

So Mrs. Gribble decided not to call her new daughter Nocticula or Valpurgina and settled for Odge (which rhymed with splodge) and hoped that she would improve as she grew older.

And up to a point, Odge did get a little more haglike. She had unequal eyes: the left one was green and the right one was brown, and she had one blue tooth—but it was a molar and right at the back; the kind you only see when you're at the dentist. There was also a bump on one of her feet which just could have been the beginning of an extra toe, though not a very big one.

Nothing is worse than knowing you have failed your

parents, but Odge did not whinge or whine. She was a strong-willed little girl with a chin like a prizefighter's and long black hair which she drew like a curtain when she didn't want to speak to anyone, and she was very independent. What she liked best was to wander along the seashore making friends with the mistmakers and picking up the treasures that she found there.

It was on one of these lonely walks that she came across the Nurse's Cave.

It was a big, dark cave with water dripping from the

walls, and the noise that came from it made Odge's blood run cold. Dreadful moans, frightful wails, shuddering sobs . . . She stopped to listen, and after a while she heard that the wails had words to them, and that there seemed to be not one wailing voice but three.

"Ooh," she heard. "Oooh, *ooh* . . . I shall never forgive myself. Never!"

"Never, never!" wailed the second voice.

"I deserve to die," moaned a third.

Odge crossed the sandy bay and entered the cave. Three women were sitting there, dressed in the uniform of nursery nurses. Their hair was plastered with ashes, their faces were smeared with mud—and as they wailed and rocked, they speared pieces of completely burnt toast from a smoldering fire and put them into their mouths.

"What's the matter?" asked Odge.

"What's the *matter?*" said the first woman. Odge could see that she had red hair beneath the ashes and a long, freckled nose.

"What's the MATTER?" repeated the second one, who looked so like the first that Odge realized she had to be her sister.

"How is that you don't know about our sorrow and our guilt?" said the third—and she too was so alike that Odge knew they must be triplets.

Then Odge remembered who they were. The tragedy

had happened before she was born, but even now the Island was still in mourning.

"Are you the nurses who took the Prince Up There and allowed him to be stolen?"

"We are," said one of the women. She turned furiously to her sister. "The toast is not burnt enough, Lily. Go and burn it some more."

Then Odge heard how they had lived in the cave ever since that dreadful day so as to punish themselves. How they ate only food that was burnt or moldy or so stale that it hurt their teeth and never anything they were fond of, like bananas. How they never cleaned their teeth or washed, so that fleas could jump into their clothes and bite them, and always chose the sharpest stones to sleep on so that they woke up sore and bruised.

"What happened to the Prince after he was stolen?" asked Odge. She was much more interested in the stolen baby than in how bruised the nurses were or how disgusting their food was.

"He was snatched by an evil woman named Mrs. Trottle and taken to her house."

"How do you know that," asked Odge, "if the door in the gump was closed?" (Hags do not start school till they are eight years old, so she still had a lot to learn.)

"There are those who can pass through the gump even when it is shut, and they told us."

"Ghosts, do you mean?"

Violet nodded. "My foot feels comfortable," she grumbled. "I must go and dip it in the icy water and turn my toes blue."

"What did she do with him? With the baby?"

"She pretended he was her own son. He lives with her now. She has called him Raymond Trottle."

"Raymond Trottle," repeated Odge. It seemed an unlikely name for a prince. "And he's still living there and going to school and everything? He doesn't know who he is?"

"That's right," said Rose, poking a stick into her ear so as to try and draw blood. "But in two years from now, the gump will open and the rescuers will go and bring him back and then we will stop wailing and eating burnt toast and our feet will grow warm and the sun will shine on our faces."

"And the Queen will smile again," said Lily.

"Yes, that will be best of all, when the Queen smiles properly once more."

Odge was very thoughtful as she made her way back along the shore, taking care not to step on the toes of the mistmakers who lay basking on the sand. The Prince was only four months older than she was. How did he feel, being Raymond Trottle and living in the middle of London? What would he think when he found out that he wasn't who he thought he was?

And who would be chosen to bring him back? The

rescuers would be famous; they would go down in history.

"I wish I could go," thought Odge, nudging her blue tooth with her tongue. "I wish *I* could be a rescuer."

Already she felt that she knew the Prince; that she would like him for a friend.

Suddenly she stopped. She set her jaw. "I *will* go," she said aloud. "I'll make them let me go."

From that day on, Odge was a girl with a mission. She started school the following year and worked so hard that she was soon top of her class. She jogged, she threw boulders around to strengthen her biceps, she studied maps of London, and tried to cough up frogs. And a month before the gump was due to open, she wrote a letter to the palace.

When you have worked and worked for something, it is almost impossible to believe that you can fail. Yet when the names of the rescuers were announced, Odge Gribble's name was not among them.

It was the most bitter disappointment. She would have taken it better if the people who *had* been chosen were mighty and splendid warriors who would ride through the gump on horseback, but they were not. A wheezing old wizard, a slightly batty fey, and a one-eyed giant who lived in the mountains moving goats about and making cheese . . .

The head teacher, when she announced who was going in Assembly, had given the reason.

"Cornelius the Wizard has been chosen because he is *wise*. Gurkintrude the fey has been chosen because she is *good*. And the giant Hans has been chosen because he is *strong*."

Of course, being the head teacher, she had then gone on to tell the children that if they wanted to do great deeds when they were older, they must themselves remember to be wise and good and strong, and they could begin by getting their homework done on time and keeping their classroom tidy.

When you are a hag it is important not to cry, but Odge, as she sat on a rock that evening wrapped in her hair, was deeply and seriously hurt.

"I am wise," she said to herself. "I was top again in algebra. And I'm strong: I threw a boulder right across Anchorage Bay. As for being good, I can't see any point in that—not for a mission which might be dangerous."

And yet the letter she had written to the King and Queen had been answered by a secretary who said he felt Miss Gribble was too young.

Sitting alone by the edge of the sea, Odge Gribble ground her teeth.

But there was another reason why those three people had been chosen. The King and Queen wanted their son to be brought back quietly. The didn't want to unloose a lot of strange and magical creatures on the city of London—creatures who would do sensational tricks and be noticed. They dreaded television crews getting excited and newspapermen writing articles about a Lost Continent or a Stolen Prince. As far as the Island was a Lost Continent, they wanted it to stay that way, and they were determined to protect their son from the kind of fuss that went on Up There when anything unusual was going on.

So they had chosen rescuers who could do magic if it was absolutely necessary but could pass for human beings—well, more or less. Of course, if anything went wrong, they had hordes of powerful creatures in reserve: winged harpies with ghastly claws; black dogs that could bay and howl over the rooftops; monsters with pale, flat eyes who could disguise themselves as rocks. . . . All these could be sent through the tunnel if the Trottles turned nasty, but no one expected this. The Trottles had done a dreadful thing; they would certainly be sorry and give up the child with good grace.

Yet now, as the rescuers stood in the drawing room of the palace ready to be briefed, the King and Queen did feel a pang. Cornelius was the mightiest wizard on the Island; a man so learned that he could divide twenty-three-thousand-seven-hundred-and-forty-one by six-and-three-quarters in the time it took a cat to sneeze. He could change the weather and strike fire from a rock, and what was most important, he had once been a university professor and lived Up There so that he could be made to look human without any trouble. Well, he *was* human.

But they hadn't realized he was quite so old. Up in his hut in the hills one didn't notice it so much, but in the strong light that came in from the sea, the liver spots on his bald pate did show up rather, and the yellowish streaks in his long white beard. Cor's neck wobbled as if holding up that domed, brain-filled head was too much for it. You could hear his bones creaking like old timbers every time he moved, and he was very deaf.

But when they suggested that he might find the journey too much, he had been deeply offended.

"To bring back the Prince will be the crowning glory of my life," he'd said.

"And I'll be there to help him," Gurkintrude had promised, looking at the old man out of her soft blue eyes.

"I know you will, dear," said the Queen, smiling at her favorite fey. And indeed, Gurkintrude had already brought up a little patch of hair on the wizard's bald head so as to keep him warm for the journey. True, it looked more like grass because she was a sort of growth goddess, a kind of agricultural fairy, but the wizard had been very pleased.

If the Queen couldn't go herself to fetch back her son (and the Royal Advisors had forbidden it), there was no one she would rather have sent than this fruitful and loving person. Flowers sprang from the ground for Gurkie, trees put out their leaves—and she never forgot the vegetables either. It was because of what she did for those rich, swollen things like marrows and pumpkins—and in particular for those delicious, tiny cucumbers called gherkins which taste so wonderful when pickled —that her name (which had been Gertrude) had gradually changed the way it had.

And Gurkintrude, too, would be at home in London because her mother had been a gym mistress in a girls' school and had run about in gray shorts shouting, "Well Played!" and "Spiffing!" before she came to the Island. Gurkie had adored her mother, and she sometimes talked to her plants as though they were the girls of St. Agnes School, crying, "Well grown!" to the raspberries or telling a lopsided tree to "Pull Your Socks Up and Play the Game."

The third rescuer was lying behind a screen being tested by the doctor. Hans was an ogre—a one-eyed giant—a most simple and kindly person who lived in the mountains putting things right for the goats, collecting feathers for his alpine hat, and yodeling.

As giants go he was not very big, but anyone bigger would not have been able to get through the door of the gentlemen's cloakroom. Even so, at a meter taller than an ordinary person, he would have been noticed, so it had been decided to make him invisible for the journey.

This was no problem. Fernseed, as everyone knows, makes people invisible in a moment, but just a few people can't take it on their skin. They come out in lumps and bumps or develop a rash, and it was to test the ogre's skin that the doctor had taken him behind the screen. Now he came out, carrying his black bag and beaming.

"All is well, Your Majesties," he said. "There will be no ill effects at all."

Hans followed shyly. The ogre always wore leather shorts with embroidered braces, and they could see on his huge pink thigh a patch of pure, clear nothingness.

But he was looking a little worried.

"My eye?" he said. "I wish not seed in my eye?" (He spoke in short sentences and with a foreign accent because his people, long ago, had come through a gump in the Austrian Alps.)

Everyone understood this. If you have only one eye, it really matters.

"I don't think anyone will notice a single eye floating so high in the air," said the Chief Advisor. "And if they do, he could always shut it."

So this was settled and the Palace Secretary handed Cornelius a map of the London Underground and a

briefcase full of money. There was always plenty of that because the people who came through the gump brought it to the treasury, not having any use for it on the Island, and the King now gave his orders.

"You know already that no magic must be used directly on the Prince," he said—and the rescuers nodded. The King and Queen liked ruling over a place where unusual things happened, but they themselves were completely human and could only manage if they kept magic strictly out of their private lives. "As for the rest, I think you understand what you have to do. Make your way quietly to the Trottles' house and find the so-called Raymond. If he is ready to come at once, return immediately and make your way down the tunnel, but if he needs time—"

"How could he?" cried the Queen. "How could he need time?" The thought that her son might not want to come to her at once hurt her so much that she had to catch her breath.

"Nevertheless, my dear, it may be a shock to him, and if so," he turned back to the rescuers, "you have a day or two to get him used to the idea, but whatever you do, don't delay more than—"

He was interrupted by a knock on the door, and a palace servant entered.

"Excuse me, Your Majesties, but there is someone waiting at the gates. She has been here for hours, and though I have explained that you are busy, she simply will not go away."

"Who is it?" asked the Queen.

"A little girl, Your Majesty. She has a suitcase full of sandwiches and a book and says she will wait all night if necessary."

The King frowned. "You had better show her in," he said.

Odge entered and bobbed a curtsey. She looked grim and determined and carried a suitcase with the words ODGE GRIBBLE—HAG painted on the side.

The Queen smiled—almost a proper smile now that she was soon to see her son. "Aren't you Mrs. Gribble's youngest?" she said in her soft voice.

"Yes, I am."

"And what can we do for you, my dear? Your sisters are well, I trust?"

Odge scowled. Her sisters were very well, showing off, shrieking, flapping, digging the garden with their long fingernails, and generally making her feel bad. But this was no time for her own problems.

"I want you to let me go with the rescuers and fetch the Prince," said Odge. "I wrote a letter about it."

The King's secretary now stepped forward and said that Miss Gribble had indeed offered her services, but he had felt that her youth made her unsuitable.

The King nodded and the Queen said gently: "You *are* too young, my dear—you must see that yourself."

"I'm the same age as the Prince," said Odge. "Almost. And I think it would be nice for him to have someone young."

"The rescuers have already been chosen, " said the King.

"Yes, I know. But I don't take up much room. And I think I know how he might feel. Raymond Trottle, I mean."

"How?" asked the Queen eagerly.

"Well, a bit muddled. I mean, he thinks he's a Trottle and he thinks Mrs. Trottle is his mother and—"

"But she isn't! She isn't! She's a wicked woman and a thief."

"Yes, that's true," said Odge. "But if he's a royal prince, it will be difficult for him to hate his mother and—" She broke off, not wanting to say more.

"It could be a dangerous journey," said the Queen.

Odge drew herself up to her full height, which was not very great. Her green eye glinted and her brown eye glared. "I am a hag," she said huffily. "I am Odge-with-the-Tooth." She stepped forward and opened her mouth very wide, and the Queen could indeed see a glimmer of blue right at the back. "Darkness and Danger is meat and drink to hags."

The King and Queen knew this to be true—but it

was absurd to send such a little girl. It was out of the question.

"Sometimes I cough frogs," said Odge—and blushed because it wasn't true. Once she had coughed something that she thought might be a tadpole, but it hadn't been.

"Why do you want to go?" asked the King.

"I just want to," said Odge. "I want to so much that I feel it must be *meant*."

There was a long pause. Then the Queen said: "Odge, if you were allowed to go, what would you say to the Prince when you first saw him?"

"I wouldn't *say* anything," said Odge. "I'd bring him a present."

"What kind of a present?" asked the King.

Odge told him.

CHAPTER 4

"WELL, THIS IS IT!" said Ernie Hobbs, floating past the boarded-up Left-Luggage Office and coming to rest on an old mailbag. "This is the day!"

He was a thin ghost with a drooping moustache, still dressed in the railway porter's uniform he'd worn when he worked in the station. Ernie hated the newfangled luggage trolleys, taking the bread out of the mouths of honest men who used to carry people's suitcases. He also had a sorrow because, after he died, his wife had married again, and when he went to haunt his old house, Ernie could see a man called Albert Fisher sitting in Ernie's old chair with a napkin tied round his nasty neck, eating the bangers and mash that Ernie's wife had cooked for him.

All the same, Ernie was a hero. It was he who had seen Mrs. Trottle snatch the baby Prince outside the fish shop and tried to glide after the Rolls-Royce and stop her—and when that hadn't worked, he'd bravely floated through the gump (although wind tunnels do awful things to the stuff that ghosts are made of) and brought the dreadful news to the sailors waiting in the Cove.

Since then, for nine long years, Ernie and the other station ghosts had kept watch on the Trottles' house, and now they waited to welcome the rescuers and show them the way.

"Are you going to say anything?" asked Mrs. Partridge. "About . . . you know . . . Raymond?"

She was an older ghost than Ernie and remembered the war and how friendly everyone had been, with the soldiers crowding the station and always ready for a chat. Being a specter suited her: her legs had been dreadful when she was alive—all swollen and sore from scrubbing floors all day, and she never got over feeling as free and light as air.

Ernie shook his head. "Don't think so," he said. "No point in upsetting them. They'll find out soon enough."

Mrs. Partridge nodded. She never believed in making

trouble—and a very pale, frail ghost called Miriam Hughes-Hughes agreed. She'd been an apologizing lady—one of those people whose voices come over the loudspeaker all day saying "sorry" to travelers because their trains are late. No one can do that for long and stay healthy, and she had died quite young of sadness and pneumonia.

They were a close band, the specters who haunted Platform Thirteen. The Ghosts of the Gump, they called themselves, and they didn't have much truck with outsiders. There was the ghost of a train spotter called Brian who'd got between the buffers and the 9:15

from Peterborough, and the ghost of the old woman who'd lost her umbrella and still hovered over the Left-Luggage Office keeping an eye on it. . . . And there were others haunting shyly in various parts of the station, not wanting to put themselves forward, but ready to lend a hand if they were needed.

The hands of the great clock moved slowly forward.

Not the clock on Platform Thirteen, which was covered in cobwebs, but that of the main one. Eleven-thirty . . . eleven forty-five . . . midnight . . .

And then it happened! The wall of the gentlemen's cloakroom moved slowly, slowly to one side. A hole appeared . . . a deep, dark hole . . . and from it came swirls of mist and, very faintly, the smell of the sea. . . .

Mrs. Partridge clutched Ernie's arm. "Oooh, I am excited!" she whispered.

And indeed it was exciting; it was awesome. The dark hole, the swirling mist . . . and now in the hole there appeared . . . figures. Three of them . . . and hovering high above them, a clear blue eye.

"Welcome!" said Ernie Hobbs. He bowed, the women curtsied.

And the rescuers stepped forward into the light.

It has to be said that the ghosts were surprised. They knew that the Prince was to be brought back without a fuss, but they had expected . . . well . . . something a bit fiercer.

Of course they could see that the ancient gentleman now tottering toward them was a wizard. His face was very wise, and there seemed to be astrological signs on his long, dark cloak, though when they looked more carefully they saw they were pieces of very old spaghetti in tomato sauce. The wizard's ear trumpet, which he

wore on a string around his neck, had tangled with the
cord holding his spectacles so that it looked as if he
might choke to death before he ever set out on his mission, and though they could see a place on his shoulder
where a mighty eagle must have once perched, it was
definitely not there anymore. Yet when he came forward
to shake hands with them, the ghosts were impressed.
How you shake hands with a ghost matters, because of
course you feel nothing, and someone who isn't a true
gentleman can just wave his hands about in midair and
make a ghost feel really small.

"I am Cornelius the Mighty," said Cor, "and I bring
thanks from Their Majesties for your Guardianship of
the Gump."

He then introduced Gurkintrude.

The fey was wearing a large hat decorated with
flowers, but also with a single beetroot. It was a living
beetroot—Gurkie would never have worn anything that
was dead—and she carried a basket full of important
things for gardening: a watering can, some brown paper
bags, a roll of twine. . . . The ghosts knew all about
these healing ladies who go about making things better
for everyone, and they had seen fairy godmothers in the
pantomime, but Mrs. Partridge was a bit worried about
the hat. The beetroot suited Gurkie—it went with her
kind pink face—but of course vegetables are not worn
very much in London.

But it was the third person who puzzled the Ghosts of the Gump particularly. Why had the rulers of the Island sent a little girl?

Odge's thick black hair had been yanked into two pigtails, and she wore a pleated gym slip and a blazer with "Play Up and Play the Game" embroidered on the pocket. The uniform was an exact copy of the one that the girls of St. Agnes wore in the photograph that Gurkie's mother had had on her mantelpiece, but the ghosts did not know that—nor did they understand why the suitcase she was clutching, holding it out in front of her like a tea tray, was punched full of holes.

Fortunately the Eye at least belonged to the kind of rescuer they had expected. Because they themselves were often invisible, the ghosts could make out the shape of the ogre even though he was covered in fern-seed. They could see his enormous muscles, each the size of a young sheep, and his sledgehammer fists, and while the embroidered braces were a pity, they thought that he would do very well as a bodyguard.

Cornelius now explained that they were disguised as an ordinary human family. "I am a retired university professor, Gurkintrude is my niece who works for the Ministry of Agriculture, and Odge is her goddaughter on the way to boarding school." As for the ogre, he told them, he would stay invisible, closing his eye when necessary but not, it was hoped, bumping into things.

"And the dear boy?" Gurkintrude now asked eagerly. "Dear little Raymond? He is well?"

There was a pause while Ernie and Mrs. Partridge looked at each other, and the ghost of the apologizing lady stared at the ground.

"He's very well," said Ernie.

"In the pink," put in Mrs. Partridge.

"And knows nothing?"

"Nothing," agreed Ernie.

It now struck the rescuers that there was very little bustle round the gentlemen's cloakroom and that this was unusual. Last time the gump had opened there'd been a stream of people going down: tree spirits whose trees had got Dutch elm disease, water nymphs whose ponds had dried up, and just ordinary people who were fed up with the pollution and the noise. But when they pointed this out to Ernie, he said: "Maybe they'll come later. There's nine days to go."

Actually, he didn't think they'd come later. He didn't think they'd come at all, and he knew why.

"Let us plunge into the bowels of the earth," said Cornelius who wanted to be on his way.

But the Underground had stopped running and so had the buses. "And I wouldn't advise waking Raymond Trottle in the middle of the night," said Ernie. "I wouldn't advise that at all!"

So it was decided they would walk to Trottle Towers

and rest in the park till morning. There was a little summer house hidden in the bushes, close to Raymond's back door where nobody would find them. The only problem was the wizard, who was too tottery to go far, and the giant solved that by saying: "I pig him on back."

This seemed a good idea. Of course they'd have to watch out for people who'd be surprised to see an old gentleman having a piggyback in midair, but as the ghosts were coming along to show them the way, that wouldn't be difficult.

Odge had gone back into the cloakroom to do something to her suitcase. They could hear a tap running and her voice talking to someone. Now, as she stomped after the others down the platform, Ernie took a closer look at her—at the unequal eyes, the fierce black eyebrows which met in the middle . . . and a glimmer of blue as she yawned.

Not just a little girl, then. A hag. Well, they could do with one of those with what was coming to them, thought Ernie Hobbs.

"Goodness, isn't it grand!" said Gurkintrude, looking at the house, which was as famous on the Island as Buckingham Palace or the castle where King Arthur had lived with his knights.

Gurkie was right. Trottle Towers was *very* grand. It had three stories and bristled with curly bits of plasterwork and bow windows and turrets in the roof. The front of the house was separated from the street by a stony garden with gravel paths and a high spiked gate. On the railings were notices saying TRADESMEN NOT ADMITTED and IT IS STRICTLY FORBIDDEN TO PARK— and on the brickwork of the house were three burglar alarms like yellow boils.

The back of the house faced the park, and it was from here that the rescuers had come. The ghosts had returned to the gump. Dawn was just breaking, but inside the house everything was silent and dark.

Then as they stood and looked, a light came on downstairs, deep in the basement. The room had barred windows and almost no furniture so that they could see who was inside as clearly as on a stage.

A boy.

A boy with light hair and a friendly, intelligent face. He was dressed in jeans and a sweater—and he was working. On a low table stood a row of shoes—shoes of all shapes and sizes: boots and ladies' high-heeled sandals and gentlemen's laceups—and the boy was cleaning them. Not just rubbing a cloth over them, but working in the polish with a will—and as he worked, he whistled; they could just hear him through the open slit at the top of the window.

And the rescuers turned to each other and smiled, for they could see that the Prince had been taught to

work; that he wasn't being brought up spoilt and selfish as they had feared. Something about the way the ghosts had spoken about Raymond Trottle had worried them, but the boy's alert face, the willing way in which he polished other people's shoes, was a sign of the best possible breeding. This was a prince who would know how to serve others, as did his parents.

The boy finished the shoes and carried them out. A second light went on, and they saw him enter a scullery, fill a kettle, and lay out some cups and saucers on a tray. This job too he did neatly and nimbly, and Odge sighed, for it was amazing how right she had been about the

Prince; he was just the kind of person she wanted for a friend, and she held on even tighter to the suitcase, glad that she had brought him the best present that any boy could have.

The scullery light went off, and a light appeared between the crack in a pair of curtains which the boy now drew back. As he did this, they could see his face turned toward them: the straight, light hair lapping the level brows, the wide-set eyes and the pointed chin. Then he made his way to the bed and set the tray down beside a fierce-looking lady who didn't seem to be thanking him at all, but just grabbed her cup.

"That must be Mrs. Trottle," whispered Gurkintrude. "She doesn't look very loving."

The boy's tasks were still not done. Back in the scullery, he took out a mop and a bucket and began to wipe the floor. Was he perhaps working a little *too* hard for a child who had not yet had breakfast? Or was he on a training scheme? Knights often lived like this before a joust or a tournament—and boy scouts, too.

But nothing mattered except that the Prince was everything a boy should be and that the day they brought him back to his rightful home would be the most joyful one the Island had ever known.

"Can't we go and tell him we're here?" asked Odge.

There was no need. The boy had come out of the back door carrying a polythene bag full of rubbish which he put in the dustbin. Then he lifted his head and saw them. For a moment he stood perfectly still with a look of wonder on his face, and it was almost as though he was listening to some distant, remembered music. Then he ran lightly up the basement steps and threw open the gate.

"Can I help you?" he asked. "Is there anyone you want to see?"

Cor the Wise stepped forward. He wanted to greet the Prince by his true name, to bow his head before him, but he knew he must not startle him, and trying to speak in an ordinary voice (though he was very much moved) he said: "Yes, there is someone we want to see. You."

The boy drew in his breath. He looked at Gurkie's round, kind face, at the grassy patch on the wizard's head, at Odge who had turned shy and was scuffing her shoes. Then he sighed, as though a weight had fallen from him, and said: "You mean it? It's really me you've come to see?"

"Indeed it is, my dear," said Gurkintrude and put her arm round him. He was too thin and why hadn't Mrs. Trottle cut his hair? It was bothering him, flopping over his eyes.

The boy's next words surprised them. "I wish I could ask you in, but I'm not allowed to have visitors," he said—and they could see how much he minded not being able to invite them to his house. "But there's a bench there under the oak tree where you could rest, and I could get you a drink. No one's up yet, they wouldn't notice."

"We need nothing," said Cor. "But let us be seated. We have much to tell you."

They made their way back into the park, and the boy took out his handkerchief and wiped the wooden slats of the seat clear of leaves. It was as though he was inviting them to his bench even if he couldn't invite them to his house. Nor would he himself sit down, but stood before them and answered their questions in a steady voice.

"You have lived all your life in Trottle Towers?" asked Cor.

"Yes." A shadow spread for a moment over his face as though he was looking back on a childhood that had been far from happy.

"And you have learnt to work, we can see that. But your schooling?"

"Oh, yes; I go to school. It's across the park in a different part of London."

Very different, he thought. Swalebottle Junior was in a rowdy, shabby street; the building was full of cracks and the teachers were often tired, but it was a good place to be. It was the holidays he minded, not the term.

The ogre had managed to follow them to the bench

with his eye shut, but the Prince's voice pleased him so much that he now opened it. Cor frowned at him, Gurkie shook her head—they had been so careful not to startle the Prince, and invisible ogres *are* unusual; there is nothing to be done about that. But the boy didn't seem at all put out by a single blue eye floating halfway up the trunk of the tree.

"Is he . . . or she . . . I don't want to pry, but is he a friend of yours?"

Hans was introduced, and the visitors made up their minds. The Prince was entirely untroubled by magic; it was as though the traditions of the Island were in his blood even if he hadn't been there since he was three months old. It was time to reveal themselves and take him back.

"Was that Mrs. Trottle to whom you brought a cup of tea?" asked Cor. "Because we have something to say to her."

The boy smiled. "Oh, goodness, no!" he said. "Mrs. Trottle lives upstairs. That was the cook."

Cor frowned. He was an old-fashioned man and a bit of a snob, and he did not think it absolutely right that a prince should have to take morning tea to the cook.

But Odge had had enough of talking.

"I've brought you something," she said in her abrupt, throaty little voice. "A present. Something nice."

She put the suitcase down on the grass. The words

ODGE GRIBBLE—HAG had been painted out. Instead she'd written THIS WAY UP. HANDLE WITH CARE.

The boy crouched down beside her. He could hear the present breathing through the holes. Something alive, he thought, his eyes alight.

It was at this moment that, on the first floor of Trottle Towers, someone began to scream.

All of them were used to the sound of screaming. Odge's sisters practically never stopped, banshees wailed through the trees of the Island, harpies yowled, and the sound of bull seals calling to their mates sometimes seemed to shake the rafters. But this was not that sort of a scream. It was not the healthy scream of someone going about their business; it was a whining, self-pitying, blackmailing sort of scream. Odge refastened the catch of her suitcase in a hurry; Gurkintrude put her arm round the Prince, and the Eye soared upward as Hans got to his feet.

"What is it, dear boy?" asked Gurkie, and put her free hand up to her head as though to protect the beet-root from the dreadful noise.

"Is it someone having an operation?" said Cornelius. "I thought you had anesthetics?"

The boy shook his head. "No," he said. "It's nothing like that. It's Raymond."

A terrible silence fell.

"What do you mean, it's Raymond?" asked Cor when he could speak again. "Surely you are Raymond Trottle, the supposed son of Mr. and Mrs. Trottle?"

The boy shook his head once more. "No. Oh, goodness, no! I'm only the kitchen boy. I'm not anybody. My name is Ben."

As he spoke, Ben moved away and stood with his back to the visitors. It was over, then. It wasn't him they'd come to see; he'd been an idiot. When he'd seen them standing there he'd had such a feeling of . . . homecoming, as though at last the years of drudgery were over. It was like that dream he had sometimes—the dream with the sea in it, and soft green turf, and someone whose face he couldn't see clearly, but who he knew wanted him.

Only dreams were things you woke from, and he should have known that it was not him but Raymond the visitors had come to find. Everything had always belonged to Raymond. All his life he'd been used to Raymond living upstairs with everything he wished for and parents to dote on him. Raymond had cupboards full of toys he never even looked at and more clothes than he knew what to do with; he was driven to his posh school in a Rolls-Royce, and just to tear the wrapping paper from his Christmas presents took Raymond hours.

And so far Ben hadn't minded. He was used to living with the servants, used to sleeping in a windowless cupboard and working for his keep. You couldn't envy Raymond, who was always whining and saying: "I'm bored!"

But this was different. That these strange, mysterious, interesting people belonged to Raymond and not to him was almost more than he could bear.

"You're sure he isn't being tortured?" asked Cor as the screams went on.

"Quite sure. He often does it."

"*Often?*" said the wizard and shook out his ear trumpet in case he had misheard.

Ben nodded. "Whenever he doesn't want to go to school. Probably he hasn't done his homework. I usually do it for him, but I couldn't yesterday because I was visiting my grandmother in hospital."

"Who is your grandmother?" Odge wanted to know.

"She's called Nanny Brown. She used to be Mrs. Trottle's Nanny, and she still lives here in the basement. She adopted me when I was a baby because I didn't have any parents."

"What happened to them?"

Ben shrugged. "I don't know. They died. Mr. Fulton thinks they must have been in prison because Nanny never mentions them."

Talking about Nanny Brown was difficult because

she was very ill. It was she who protected him from the bullying of the servants—even the snooty butler, Mr. Fulton, respected her—and if she died . . .

The rescuers were silent, huddled together on the bench. Hans had closed his eye and was covering his face with his invisible hand. He was used to the silence of the mountains and felt a headache coming on. Odge was crouched over the suitcase as though to comfort what was inside.

It was a *child* who was making that noise; the child they had come so far to find. And the boy they liked so much had nothing to do with them at all!

CHAPTER 5

WHAT IS IT, my angel, my babykins, my treasure?" said Mrs. Trottle, coming into the room.

She had been making up her face when Raymond's screams began. Now her right cheek was covered in purple rouge, and her left cheek was still a rather nasty gray color. Mrs. Trottle's hair was in curlers, and she gave off a strong smell of Maneater because she always went to bed covered in scent.

Raymond continued to scream.

"Tell Mama; tell your Mummy, my pinkyboo," begged Mrs. Trottle.

"I've got a pain in my tummy," yelled Raymond. "I'm ill."

Mrs. Trottle pulled back the covers on Raymond's huge bed with its padded headboard and the built-in switches for his television set, his two computers, and

his electric trains. She put a finger on Raymond's stomach, and the finger vanished because Raymond was extremely fat.

"Where does it hurt, my pettikins? Which bit?"

"Everywhere," screeched Raymond. "All over!"

Since Raymond had eaten an entire box of chocolates the night before, this was not surprising, but Mrs. Trottle looked worried.

"I can't go to school!" yelled Raymond, getting to the point. "I can't!"

Raymond's school was the most expensive in London; the uniform alone cost hundreds of pounds, but he hated it.

"Of course you can't, my lambkin," said Mrs. Trottle, drawing her finger out of Raymond's middle. "I'll send a message to the headmaster. And then I'll call a doctor."

"No, no—not the doctor! I don't want the doctor; he makes me worse," yelled Raymond—and indeed the doctor was not always as kind to darling Raymond as he might have been.

Mr. Trottle now came in looking cross because he had sat on his portable telephone again and asked what was the matter.

"Our little one is ill," said Mrs. Trottle. "You must tell Willard to drive to the school after he has dropped you at the bank and let them know."

"He doesn't look ill to me," said Mr. Trottle—but he

never argued with his wife, and anyway he was in a hurry to go and lend a million pounds to a property developer who wanted to cover a beautiful Scottish island with holiday homes for the rich.

Raymond's screams grew less. They became wails, then snivels . . .

"I feel a bit better now," he said. "I might manage some breakfast." He had heard the car drive away and knew that the danger of school was safely past.

"Perhaps a glass of orange juice?" suggested Mrs. Trottle.

"No. Some bacon and some sausages and some fried bread," said Raymond.

"But, darling—"

Raymond puckered up his face, ready to scream again.

"All right, my little sugar lump. I'll tell Fulton. And then a quiet day in bed."

"No. I don't want a quiet day. I feel better now. I want to go to lunch at Fortlands. And then shopping. I want a laser gun like Paul has at school, and a knife, and—"

"But, darling, you've already got seven different guns," said Mrs. Trottle, looking at Raymond's room, which was completely strewn with toys he had pushed aside or broken or refused to put away.

"Not like the one Paul's got—not a sonic-trigger activated laser, and I want one. I *want* it."

"Very well, dear," said Mrs. Trottle. "We'll go to lunch at Fortlands. You do look a little rosier."

This was true. Raymond looked very rosy indeed. People usually do when they have yelled for half an hour.

"And shopping?" asked Raymond. "Not just lunch but shopping afterward?"

"And shopping," agreed Mrs. Trottle. "So now give your mumsy a great big sloppy kiss."

That was how things always ended on days when Raymond didn't feel well enough to go to school—with Raymond and Mrs. Trottle, dressed to kill, going to have lunch in London's grandest department store.

The name of the store was Fortlands and Marlow. It was in Piccadilly and sold everything you could imagine: marble bathtubs and ivory elephants and sofas that you sank into and disappeared. It had a food hall with a fountain where butlers in hard hats bought cheeses that cost a week's wages, and a bridal department where the daughters of duchesses were fitted for their wedding gowns—and none of the dresses had price tickets on them in case people fainted clean away when they saw how much they cost.

And there was a restaurant with pink chairs and pink tablecloths in which Raymond and his mother were having lunch.

"I'll have shrimps in mayonnaise," said Raymond, "and then I'll have roast pork with crackling and Yorkshire pudding and—"

"I'm afraid the Yorkshire pudding comes with the roast beef, sir," said the waitress. "With the pork you get applesauce and red-currant jelly."

"I don't like applesauce," whined Raymond. "It's all squishy and gooey. I want Yorkshire pudding. I *want* it."

It was at this moment that the rescuers entered the store. They too were having lunch in the restaurant. When Ben had told them how Raymond was going to spend the day, they decided to follow the Prince and study him from a distance so that they could decide how best to make themselves known to him.

"Only I want Ben to come," Odge said.

Everyone wanted Ben to come, but he said he couldn't. "I don't have school today because they need the building for a council election, and I promised my grandmother I'd come to the hospital at dinnertime."

But he said he would go with them as far as Fortlands and point Raymond out because the Trottles had gone off in the Rolls and no one had seen him yet. Hans, though, decided to stay behind. He didn't like crowded places, and he lay down under an oak tree and went to sleep, which made a great muddle for the dogs, who didn't understand why they couldn't walk through a perfectly empty patch of grass.

Gurkie absolutely loved Fortlands. The vegetable display was quite beautiful—the passion fruit and the pineapples and the cauliflowers so artistically arranged —and she had time to say nice things to a tray of broccoli which looked a little lonely. In a different sort of shop, the rescuers might have stood out, but Fortlands was full of old-fashioned people coming up from the country, and they fit in quite well. The only thing people did stare at a bit was the beetroot in Gurkie's hat, so she decided to leave it in the fountain to soak quietly while she went up to the restaurant. It was as she was bending over the water to look for a place where the beloved vegetable would not be noticed that she saw, beneath the water weed, a small, sad face.

Bending down to see more clearly, she found that she had not been mistaken.

"Yes, it's me," said a slight, silvery voice. "Melisande. I heard you were coming." And then: "I'm not a mermaid, you know, I'm a water nymph. I've got feet."

"Yes, I know, dear; I can see you've got feet. But you don't look well. What are those marks on your arms?"

"It's the coins. People chuck coins into the fountain all day long, heaven knows why. I'm all over bruises— and the water isn't changed nearly often enough."

And her lovely, tiny face really did look very melancholy.

"Why don't you come down with us, dear?" whispered Gurkintrude. "The gump's open. We could take you wrapped in wet towels; it wouldn't be difficult."

"I was going to," said the nymph sadly. "But not now. You've seen him."

"The Prince, do you mean? We haven't yet."

"Well, you will in a minute; he's just gone up in the lift. There was a lot of us going, but who wants to be ruled by *that*?"

She then agreed to hide the beetroot under a water lily leaf, and Gurkie hurried to catch up with the others. The nymph's words had upset her, but feys always think the best of people, and she was determined to look on the bright side. Even if Mrs. Trottle had spoilt Raymond a little, there would be time to put that right when he came to the Island. When children behave badly, it is nearly always the fault of those who bring them up.

"There he is," whispered Ben. "Over there, by the window."

There was a long pause.

"You're sure?" asked Cor. "There can be no mistake?"

"I'm sure," said Ben.

He then slipped away, and the rescuers were left to study the boy they had come so far to find.

"He looks . . . healthy," said Gurkintrude, trying to make the best of things.

"And well-washed," agreed the wizard. "I imagine there would be no mold behind his ears?"

Odge didn't say anything. She still carried the suitcase, holding it out flat like a tray, and had been in a very nasty temper since she discovered that Ben was not the Prince.

What surprised them most was how like his supposed mother Raymond Trottle looked. They both had the same fat faces, the same podgy noses, the same round, pale eyes. They knew, of course, that dogs often grew to be like their owners, so perhaps it was understandable that Raymond, who had lived with the Trottles since he was three months old, should look like the woman who had stolen him, but it was odd all the same.

The visitors had looked forward very much to having lunch in a posh restaurant, but the hour that followed was one of the saddest of their lives. They found a table behind a potted palm from which they could watch the Trottles without being noticed, and what they saw got worse and worse and worse. Raymond's shrimps had arrived, and he was pushing them away with a scowl.

"I don't want them," said Raymond. "They're the wrong ones. I want the bigger ones."

As far as Gurkie was concerned, there was no such thing as a wrong shrimp or a right shrimp. All shrimps were her friends, and she would have died rather than eat one, but she felt dreadfully sorry for the waitress.

"The bigger ones are prawns, sir; and I'm afraid we don't have any today."

"Don't have any *prawns*," said Mrs. Trottle in a loud voice. "Don't have any prawns in the most expensive restaurant in London!"

The waitress had been on her feet all day, her little girl was ill at home, but she kept her temper.

"If you'd just try them, sir," she begged Raymond.

But he wouldn't. The dish was taken away and Raymond decided to start with soup. "Only not with any bits in it," he shouted after the waitress. "I don't eat bits."

Poor Gurkie's kind round face was growing paler and paler. The Islanders had ordered salad and nut cutlets, but she was so sensitive that she could hear the lamb chops screaming on the neighboring tables, and the poor stiff legs of dead pheasants sticking up from people's plates made her want to cry.

Raymond's soup came and it did have bits in it—a few leaves of fresh parsley.

"I thought I asked for *clear* soup," said Mrs. Trottle. "Really, I find it quite extraordinary that you cannot bring us what we want."

The rescuers had been up all night; they were not only sad, they were tired, and because of this they forgot themselves a little. When their nut cutlets came, they were too hard for the wizard's teeth. He should have mashed them up with his fork—of course he should. Instead, he mumbled something and in a second the cutlets had turned to liquid. Fortunately no one saw, and the liquidizing spell is nothing to write home about—it was used by wizards in the olden days to turn their enemies' bones to jelly—but it was embarrassing when they were trying so hard to be ordinary. And then the sweet peas in Gurkintrude's hat started to put out tendrils without even being told so as to shield her from the sight of the Prince fishing with his fingers in the soup.

The Trottles' roast pork came next—and the kind waitress had managed to persuade the chef to put a helping of Yorkshire pudding on Raymond's plate, though anyone who knows anything about food knows that Yorkshire pudding belongs to beef and not to pork.

Raymond stared at the plate out of his round pale eyes. "I don't want roast potatoes," he said. "I want chips. Roast potatoes are boring."

"Now Raymond, dear," began his mother.

"I want *chips*. This is supposed to be my treat, and it isn't a treat if I can't have chips."

Odge had behaved quite well so far. She had glared, she had ground her teeth, but she had gone on eating her lunch. Now though, she began to have *thoughts* and the thoughts were about her sisters—and in particular about her oldest sister, Fredegonda, who was better than anyone on the Island at ill-wishing pigs.

Ill-wishing things is not all that difficult. Witch doctors do it when they send bad thoughts to people and make them sick; sometimes you can do it when you will someone not to score a goal at football and they don't. Odge had never wanted to ill-wish pigs because she liked animals, but she had sometimes wanted to ill-wish people, and now, more than anything in the world, she wanted to ill-wish Raymond Trottle.

But she didn't. For one thing she wasn't sure if she could, and anyway she had promised to behave like the girls of St. Agnes whose uniform she wore.

"I want a Knickerbocker Glory next," said Raymond. "The kind with pink ice cream and green ice cream and jelly and peaches and raspberry juice and nuts."

The waitress went away and returned with Mrs. Trottle's caramel pudding and the Knickerbocker Glory in a tall glass. It was an absolutely marvelous one—just to look at it made Odge's mouth water.

Raymond picked up his spoon—and put it down again.

"It hasn't got an umbrella on top," he wailed. "I always have a plastic umbrella on top. I won't eat it unless I have a—Ugh! Eek! Yow! What's happened? I didn't touch it, I didn't, I *didn't*!"

He was telling the truth for once, but nobody believed him. For the Knickerbocker Glory had done a somersault and landed facedown on the table, so that the three kinds of ice cream, the jelly, the tinned

peaches, and the raspberry juice were running down
Raymond's trousers, into his socks, across his flashy
shoes . . .

Odge had not ill-wished Raymond Trottle. She had
been very good and held herself in, but not completely.
She had ill-wished the Knickerbocker Glory.

CHAPTER 6

I WANT SOME BRANDY for my teeth," said Nanny Brown.

She lay in the second bed from the end in Ward Three of the West Park Hospital, in a flannel nightdress with a drawstring round the neck because she didn't believe in showing bits of herself to the doctors. She had been old when Mrs. Trottle persuaded her to come to Switzerland with the stolen baby, and now she was very old indeed; shriveled and tired and ready to go because she'd said her prayers every day of her life, and if God wasn't waiting to take her up to heaven she'd want to know the reason why. But she was cross about her teeth.

"Now, Mrs. Brown," said the nurse briskly, "you know we can't let you soak your teeth in that nasty stuff. Just pop them in that nice glass of disinfectant."

"It isn't nice, it's smelly," grumbled Mrs. Brown. "I've always soaked my teeth in brandy, and then I drink the brandy. That's how I get my strength."

And she had needed her strength, living in the Trottles' basement helping to look after Raymond, but keeping an eye on Ben. She didn't hold with the way Larina was bringing up Raymond; she could see how spoilt he was going to be, and when he was three she'd handed him over to another nanny, but she wouldn't let Larina turn her out—not with Ben to look after. Mrs. Trottle might threaten her with the police if she said anything about the stolen baby, but the threat worked both ways. "If you turn me out, and the boy, I'll tell them everything, and who knows which of us they'll believe," Nanny Brown had said.

So she'd stayed in Trottle Towers and helped with a bit of sewing and ironing, and turned her back on what was going on in the nursery upstairs. And she'd been able to see that Ben at least was brought up properly. She couldn't stop the servants ordering him about, but she saw to his table manners and that he spoke nicely and got his schooling, and he was a credit to her.

That was the only thing that worried her—what would happen to Ben if she died. Mrs. Trottle hated Ben; she'd stop at nothing to get him sent away. But I'm going to foil her, thought Nanny Brown. Oh yes, I'm going to stop her tricks.

"There's a burglar under my bed," she said now. "I feel it. Have a look."

"Now, Mrs. Brown," said the nurse, "we don't want to get silly ideas into our head, do we?"

"It isn't silly," said Nanny peevishly. "London's full of burglars, so why not under my bed?"

The nurse wouldn't look though; she was one of the bossy ones. "What will your grandson say if you carry on like that?" she said, and walked away with her behind swinging.

But when Ben came slowly down the ward, the old woman felt better at once. She'd been strict with him: no rude words, eating up every scrap you were given, yet she didn't mind admitting that if she loved anyone in the world, it was this boy. And the other patients smiled too as he passed their beds because he was always so polite and friendly, greeting them and remembering their names.

"Hello, Nanny."

He always called her Nanny, not Grandma. She'd

told him to, it sounded better. Now he laid a small bunch of lilies of the valley down beside her, and she shook her head at him. "I told you not to waste your money." She'd left him a few pounds out of her pension when she went into hospital and told him it had to last. Waste was wicked, but her gnarled fingers closed round the bunch and she smiled.

"How are you feeling?" Ben asked.

"Oh fine, fine," lied Nanny Brown. "And you? What's been going on at home?"

Ben hesitated. He wanted to tell Nanny about his mysterious visitors, about how much he liked them . . . the strange feeling he'd had that they belonged to him. But he'd promised to say nothing and anyway he'd been wrong because they didn't belong to him. So he just said: "Nothing much. I've got onto the football team and Raymond's had another screaming fit."

"That's hardly news," said Nanny Brown grimly. And then: "No one's been bothering you? That Mr. Fulton?"

"No, not really. But . . . do you think you're coming home soon, Nanny? It's better when you're there."

Nanny patted his hand. "Bless you, of course I am. You just get on with your schooling and remember, once you're grown up, no one can tell you what to do."

"Yes."

It would be a long time though till he was a man,

and Nanny looked very ill. Fear was bad; being afraid was about yourself and you had to fight it, but just for a moment he was very much afraid whether it was selfish or not.

It was very quiet in the ward when the visitors had gone. All the other patients lay back drowsily, glad to rest, but Nanny Brown sat up in bed as fierce as a sparrow hawk. There wasn't much time to waste. And she was lucky: it was the nice nurse from the Philippines who came round to take temperatures. Celeste, she was called, and she had a lovely smile and a tiny red rose tucked into her hair behind her ear. You could only see it when she bent down, but it always made you feel better, knowing it was there.

"Listen, dear, there's something I want you to do for me. Will you get me a piece of paper and an envelope? It's really important or I wouldn't ask you."

Celeste reached for Nanny's wrist and began to take her pulse.

"I'll try, Mrs. Brown," she said. "But you'll have to wait till I've finished my rounds."

And she didn't forget. An hour later she came with the paper and a strong white envelope. "Have you got a pen?"

Nanny Brown nodded. "Thank you, dear; that's a weight off my mind. You're a good kind girl."

Celeste smiled. "That's all right." She looked closely

at the old woman's face. It wouldn't be long now. "I'll just make sure about the burglars," she said.

She bent down to look, and as she did so Nanny Brown could see the little red rose tucked in the jet black hair.

"Bless you," she said—and then, feeling much better, she began to write.

CHAPTER 7

"IS SIMPLE," said Hans. "I bop 'im. I sack 'im. We go through the gump."

The others had returned from Fortlands in such a gloomy mood that the poor ogre could hardly bear it. He'd had a good sleep and when he heard what had happened in the restaurant, he decided that he should come forward and put things right.

Cor shook his head. It was tempting to let the giant bop Raymond on the head, tie him up in a sack, and carry him back to the Island, but it couldn't be done. He imagined the King and Queen unwrapping their stunned son like a trussed piglet . . . realizing that Raymond had had to be carried off by force.

"He must come willingly, Hans," he said, "or the Queen will break her heart."

Ernie Hobbs now glided toward the little summer house where they were sitting. He usually allowed himself a breather in the early evening and had left the other ghosts in charge of the gump.

"Well, how's it going?"

The Islanders told him.

Ernie nodded. "I'm afraid it's a bad business. We've been keeping an eye on him, and he's been going downhill steadily. Mrs. Trottle's a fool and Mr. Trottle's never there—there's no one to check him."

"I suppose there can be no doubt who Raymond is?" asked Cor.

Ernie shook his head. "I saw her steal the baby. I saw her come back a year later with the baby in her arms. What's more, he had the same comforter in his mouth. I noticed it particularly with it being on a gold ring. He'll be the Prince all right."

"And what about Ben?" asked Gurkintrude.

"Ah, he's a different kettle of fish, Ben is. Been here as long as Raymond, and you couldn't find a better lad. He can see ghosts too and never a squawk out of him. The servants treat him like dirt—take their tone from

Mrs. Trottle. It'll be a bad day for the boy when his grandma dies."

He then glided off to watch Albert Fisher eat bangers and mash in his old house and make himself miserable, but first he promised the help of all the ghosts in the city if it was needed. "And not just ghosts—there's all sorts would like to see things come right on the Island," he said.

He had no sooner gone than Ben came hurrying out of the house toward them, and Odge—who had been exercising her present in the shrubbery—crawled out with her suitcase and said "Hello."

"How was your grandmother?" Gurkie asked.

A shadow crossed Ben's face. "She says she's all right but she doesn't look very well to me." And then: "How did it go at lunch?"

"Raymond was awful," said Odge. "I think he's disgusting. I think we should have a republic on the Island and not bother with a prince once the King and Queen are dead."

"*Odge!*" said Gurkie in a warning voice.

Odge hung her head. She had not meant to betray the reason for their journey any more than she had meant to ill-wish the Knickerbocker Glory, but she was a girl with strong feelings.

But Cor had come to a decision.

"I think, Ben," he said, "that you are a boy who can keep a secret?"

"Yes, sir, I am," said Ben without hesitation.

"You see, we shall need your help. You know Raymond's movements and where he sleeps and so on. So we had better explain why we are here."

He then told him about the Island, about the sorrow of the King and Queen, about their quest.

Ben listened in silence, and when they had finished, his eyes were bright with wonder. "I always knew there had to be a place like that. I knew it!" But he was amazed that Raymond had been stolen. "Mrs. Trottle's got his birth certificate framed in her room."

"Well, that just shows she's a cheat, doesn't it?" said Odge. "Who'd want to frame a crummy birth certificate unless they had something to hide?"

"Now, listen, Ben," the wizard went on, "we want you to take us to see Raymond when he's alone. Do you know when that might be?"

"Tonight would be good. The Trottles are going out and Mrs. Flint's meant to listen for him—that's the cook—but all she does is switch the telly on full blast and stay in her sitting room."

"That will do then. And now we must think how to win Raymond's trust and make him come with us. What sort of things does he like?"

This was difficult. Ben could think of a lot of things Raymond *didn't* like. After a pause he said: "Presents. He likes getting things."

"Ah, in that case—"

"*No!*" Odge broke in most rudely. She was clutching the suitcase, and her green eye gave off beams of fury. "I won't give this present to that pig of a boy."

Cornelius rose. "How *dare* you speak like that to your superiors?"

But Odge stood her ground. "This present is special. I brought it up from when it was tiny, and it's still a baby, and I'm not going to give it to Raymond because he's horrible. I'm going to give it to Ben."

Gurkintrude now knelt down beside the hag. "Look, Odge, I know how you feel. But it's our duty to bring back the Prince. The Queen trusted you as much as she trusted us, and it was because you thought of such a lovely present for her son that she said you could come. You can't let her down now."

But it was Ben who changed her mind. "If you promise to do something, Odge, then you have to do it, you know that. And if giving Raymond . . . whatever it is . . . will help, then that's part of the deal."

"Oh, all right," said Odge sulkily. "But if he doesn't treat it properly, I'll let my sisters loose on him, and that's a promise."

It was nine o'clock before the servants were settled in front of the telly and Ben could creep upstairs with his new friends.

Raymond was sitting up in bed with his boom box going full tilt, wriggling in time to the music.

"What do you want?" he said to Ben. "I don't need you. I haven't got any homework to do today because tomorrow's Saturday, and anyway you're supposed to stay in the kitchen."

"I've brought some people to see you," said Ben. "Visitors."

The rescuers entered, and Ben introduced them—all except Hans, who had to crawl through the door on his hands and knees and settled himself down with his eye shut.

Raymond stared at them. "They look funny," he said. "Are they in fancy dress?"

"No, Your Roy—" began Cor and broke off. He had been about to call Raymond "Your Royal Highness," but it was too early to reveal the full truth. "We come from another place."

"What place?" asked Raymond suspiciously.

"It's called the Island," said Gurkintrude. Feys are used to kissing children and being godmother to almost everyone, but Raymond, bulging out of his yellow silk pajamas, looked so uninviting that she had to pretend he was a vegetable marrow before she could settle down beside him on the bed. "It's a most beautiful place, Raymond. There are green fields with wildflowers growing in the grass and groves of ancient trees and rivers where the water is so clear that you can see all the stones on the bottom as if they were jewels."

Raymond didn't say anything, but at least he'd switched off his radio.

"And all round the Island are beaches of white sand and rock pools and cliffs where the seabirds come to nest each spring."

"And there are seals and buzzards and rabbits and crabs," said Odge.

"I don't like crabs," said Raymond. "They pinch you. Is there a pier with slot machines and an amusement arcade?"

"No. But you don't need an amusement arcade—the dolphins will come and talk to you, and the kelpies will take you on their backs and gallop through the waves."

"I don't believe it," said Raymond. "You're telling fibs."

"No, Raymond, it's all true," said Gurkie, "and if you come with us, we'll show you."

Cor opened his briefcase and took out a cardboard folder. "Perhaps you would like to see a picture of our King and Queen?"

He handed the photograph to Raymond. It wasn't one of the official palace portraits with the royal family in their robes. The Queen was sitting on a rock by the sea with one hand trailing in the water. Her long hair was loose, and she was smiling up at the King, who looked down at her, his face full of pride. The picture had been taken before the Prince was stolen and what came out of it most was—happiness.

"They look all right," said Raymond. "But they don't look royal. They're dressed like ordinary people. If I was royal, I'd wear a gold uniform and medals."

"Then you'd look pretty silly by the sea," said Odge, "because the salt spray would make the gold braid go all green and nasty, and your medals would clank and frighten away—"

"Now, Odge!" said Gurkie warningly.

"Could I look?" asked Ben—and Cor took the picture from Raymond and handed it to him.

Ben said nothing. He just stood looking at the photograph—looking and looking as if he could make himself part of it . . . as if he could vanish into the picture and stay there.

But now Raymond sat up very straight and pointed to the door. "Eeek!" he shouted. "There's a horrible thing there! An eye! It's disgusting; it's creepy. I want my mummy!"

The others turned their heads in dismay. They knew how sensitive the ogre was, and to call such a clean-living person "creepy" is about as hurtful as it is possible to be. And sure enough, a tear welled up in Hans' clear blue eye, trembled there . . . and fell. Then the eye vanished, and from the space where the giant sat, there came a deep, unhappy sigh.

But Odge now came to the rescue. She had promised to behave like the girls of St. Agnes who said: "Play Up and Play the Game" and she said: "Raymond, I've brought you a present, a really special one. I brought it all the way from the Island. Look!"

The word "present" cheered Raymond up at once, and he watched as she lifted her suitcase onto the bed and opened it.

"What is it?" Raymond asked.

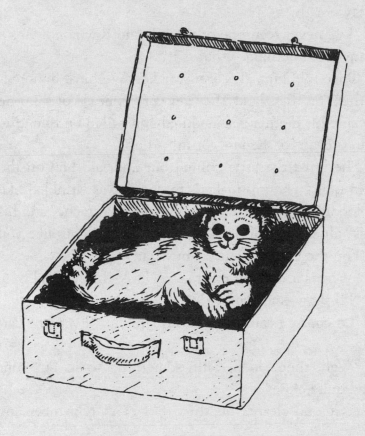

But he didn't shudder this time; he looked quite pleased. And the person who wasn't pleased with what lay inside, cradled in layers of moss, would have been made of stone. A very small animal covered in soft, snow-white fur, with big paws lightly tipped with black. His eyes, as he woke from sleep, were huge and very dark, his blob of a nose was moist and whiskery and cool, and as he looked up at Raymond and yawned, you could see his strawberry-pink tongue and smell his clean milky breath.

"I've never seen one of them," said Raymond. "It's a funny-looking thing. What is it?"

Odge told him. "It's a mistmaker. We have hundreds of them on the Island; they get very tame. I got this one because his mother got muddled and rolled on him. She didn't mean to, she just got mixed up."

She lifted the little animal out and laid him on the satin quilt. The mistmaker's forehead was wrinkled like a bloodhound's; he had a small, soft moustache, and his pink, almost human-looking ears had big lobes like you find on the ears of poets or musicians.

"Why is it called a mistmaker?" asked Raymond.

"I'll show you," said Odge. "Can you sing?"

"Of course I can sing," said Raymond. "Everyone can sing."

"Well, then, do it. Sing something to it. Put your head quite close."

Raymond cleared his throat. "I can't remember any

words," he said. "I'll play it something on my radio." He turned the knob and the room was filled with the sound of cackling studio laughter.

"You try, Ben," ordered Odge. "You sing to it."

But Ben didn't sing. He whistled. None of them had heard whistling quite like that; it was like birdsong, but it wasn't just chirruping—it had a proper tune: a soaring tune that made them think of spring and young trees and life beginning everywhere. And as Ben whistled, the little animal drew closer . . . and closer still . . . he pressed his moist nose against Ben's hands; the wrinkles on his worried-looking forehead grew smoother . . .

"Aaah," sighed the mistmaker. "Aaah . . ."

Then it began. At first there was only a little mist; he was after all very young . . . and then there came more . . . and more . . . Even from this animal only a few weeks old there came enough cool, swirling mist to wreathe Raymond's bed in whiteness. The room became beautiful and mysterious; the piles of neglected toys disappeared, and the fussy furniture . . . and the Islanders drank in the well-remembered freshness of early morning and of grass still moist with dew.

Raymond's mouth dropped open. "It's weird. I've never seen that. It isn't natural."

"Why isn't it natural?" asked Odge crossly. "Skunks make stinks and slugs make slime and people make sweat, so why shouldn't a mistmaker make mist?"

Raymond was still staring at the little creature. No

one at school had anything like that. He'd be able to show it off to everyone. Paul had a tree frog and Derek had a grass snake, but this would beat them all.

"You'd be able to play with mistmakers all day long if you came to the Island," said Gurkie. "You will come, won't you?"

"Nope," said Raymond. "I'd miss my telly and my computer games and my Scalextric set. But I'll keep him."

He made a grab for the mistmaker, but the animal had given off so much mist that he was less pillow-shaped now, and nimbler. Jumping off the bed, he landed with a thud on his nose and began to explore the room.

They watched him as he ran his whiskery moustache along Raymond's toy boxes, rolled over on the rug, rubbed himself against a chest of drawers. Sometimes he disappeared into patches of mist, then reappeared with one ear turned inside out which is what happens to mistmakers who are busy.

The wizard cleared his throat. Now was the time to come out with the truth. Such a snobby boy would surely come to the Island if he knew he would live there as a prince.

"Perhaps we should tell you, Raymond, that you are really of noble—"

He was interrupted by another and even louder shriek from Raymond.

"Look! It's lifted its leg! It's made a puddle on the carpet! It's dirty!"

Odge looked at him with loathing. "This mistmaker is *six weeks old!* They can be house-trained perfectly well but not when they are infants. You made enough puddles when you were that age, and it's a *clean* puddle. It isn't the puddle of someone who guzzles shrimps and roast pork and greasy potatoes."

Ben had already been to the bathroom for a cloth and was mopping up. Mopping up after Raymond was something he had been doing ever since he could remember. Then he gathered up the mistmaker, who was trembling all over and trying to cover his ears with his paws. You cannot be as musical as these animals are without suffering terribly from the kind of stuck-pig noises that Raymond made.

"You keep him downstairs, Ben," ordered Raymond. "You can feed him and see he doesn't mess up my room. But remember, he's *mine!*"

CHAPTER 8

ODGE AND GURKIE spent the night curled up on the floor of the little summer house. It was a pretty place with a fretwork verandah and wooden steps, but no one used it now. Years ago the roof had begun to leak, and instead of mending it, the head keeper had put up a notice saying: PRIVATE. NO ADMITTANCE. Dark privet bushes and clumps of laurel hid it from passersby. Only the animals came to it now: sparrows to preen in the lopsided birdbath; squirrels to chatter on the roof.

Nearby, a patch of snoring grass showed where the ogre rested. Ben had smuggled the mistmaker into his cupboard of a room.

But Cornelius could not sleep. He longed to conjure up a fire to keep his old bones warm, but he thought it might be noticed, and after a while he took his stick and wandered off toward the lake. The Serpentine it was called because it was wiggly and shaped like a serpent, and he remembered it from when he had lived Up Here. Londoners were fond of it; people went boating there and caught tiddlers, and brave old gentlemen broke the ice with their toes in winter and swam in it, getting goose pimples but being healthy.

But it wasn't just old men with goose pimples or lovers canoodling or children sailing their boats that came here. There were . . . others. There had been mermaids in the lake when Cor was a little boy, each tree had had its spirit, banshees had wailed in the bushes. And on Midsummer's Eve they had gathered together and had a great party.

Midsummer's Eve was in two days' time. Did they still come, the boggarts and the brownies, the nymphs and the nixies, the sproggans and the witches and the trolls? And if so, was there an idea there? If Raymond saw real magic—saw the exciting things that happened on the Island, would that persuade him to come?

Cor's ancient forehead wrinkled up in thought. Then

he raised his stick in the air and said some poetry—and seconds later Ernie Hobbs, who had been sleeping on a mail bag on Platform Thirteen of King's Cross Station, woke up and said: "Ouch!" Looking about him, he saw that Mrs. Partridge, who'd been flat out on a luggage trolley, was sitting up and looking puzzled.

"I've got a tingle in my elbow," she said. "Real fierce it is."

At the same time, Miriam Hughes-Hughes, the ghost of the apologizing lady, rolled off the bench outside the Left-Luggage Office and lay blinking on the ground.

It was Ernie who realized what had happened.

"We're being summoned! We're being sent for!"

"It'll be the wizard," said Mrs. Partridge excitedly. "There isn't no one else can do tricks like that!"

Wasting no more time, they glided down the platform and made their way to the park. They found Cornelius sitting on a tree stump and staring into the water.

"Did you call us, Your Honor?" asked Ernie.

"I did," said Cor. He then told them what had happened earlier in Raymond's room: "We went to tell him who he was, but the noise he made was more than anyone could bear. We had to leave."

The ghosts looked troubled. "We should have warned you, maybe," said Ernie, "but we thought he might be better with you."

"Well, he wasn't." Cor rubbed his aching knees. "Hans wants to bop the Prince on the head and carry him through the gump in a sack, but I think we must have another go at persuading him to come willingly. So I want you to call up all the . . . unusual people who are left Up Here and ask them to put on a special show for Raymond. Wizards, will o' the wisps . . . everyone you can find. Ask them to do the best tricks they can, and we'll build a throne for Raymond and hail him as a prince."

"A sort of Raymond Trottle Magic Show?" said Mrs. Partridge eagerly.

Ernie, though, was looking worried. "There's always a bit of a do on Midsummer's Eve, that's true enough. But . . . well, Your Honor, I don't want to throw a damper, but magic isn't what it was up here. It's what you might call the Tinkerbell Factor."

"I don't follow you," said the wizard.

"Well, there's this fairy . . . she's in a book called *Peter Pan*. Tinkerbell, she's called. When people say they don't believe in her, she goes all woozy and feeble. It's like that up here with the wizards and the witches and all. People haven't believed in them so long they've lost heart a bit."

"We can only do our best," said Cornelius. "Now, tell me, what's the situation about . . . you know . . ." He spoke quietly, not knowing who might be listening in the depths of the lake. "*Him*, the monster? Is he still there?"

"Old Nuckel? They say so," said Ernie. "But no one's

seen him for donkey's years. Have you thought of calling him up?"

"I was wondering," said Cor. "I happen to have my book of spells with me. It would make a splendid ending to the show."

The ghosts looked respectful. Raising monsters from the deep is very difficult magic indeed.

"Well, if that doesn't fetch the little perisher, nothing will," said Mrs. Partridge—and blushed, because nasty or not, Raymond Trottle was, after all, a prince.

It was incredible how helpful everyone was. Witches who worked in school kitchens trying to make two pounds of mince go round a hundred children said they would come, and so did wizards who taught chemistry and stayed behind to make interesting explosions after the children had gone home. An animal trainer who trained birds for films and television, and was really an enchanter, promised to bring his flock of white doves so that the evening could begin with a flypast.

Melisande, the water-nymph-who-was-not-a-mermaid, swam through the outlet pipe at Fortlands and spoke to her uncle who was a merrow and worked the sewers, dredging up stuff which people had flushed down the loo by mistake or lost in the plughole of the bath, and he too said he would come and do a trick for Raymond.

"Really, people are so *kind*," said Gurkie as she ran

about jollying along the tree spirits who had agreed to do a special dance for Raymond on the night.

And she was right. After all, it wasn't as though they didn't know what Raymond was like—that kind of thing gets around—but everyone wanted the King and Queen to be happy. The Island mattered to them; it was their homeland even if they themselves hadn't been there, and there seemed to be no end to the trouble they were prepared to take.

The ghosts, during these two days, were everywhere; helping, persuading, taking messages. Even Miriam Hughes-Hughes stopped apologizing and found a Ladies' Group of Banshees—those pale, ghastly women who wail and screech when something awful is going to happen, and they agreed to come and sing sad songs for the Prince. A troll called Henry Prendergast who lived in the basement of the Bank of England said he thought he could manage some shape-shifting, and Hans tried to forget the hurt that Raymond had done him by calling him creepy, and practiced weight lifting till his muscles threatened to crack. As for Odge Gribble, she went off by herself in the Underground to visit an aunt of her mother's. The aunt was an Old Woman of Gloominess and absolutely marvelous at turning people bald, and she promised to bring some friends along from her sewing circle and amuse Raymond by making donkey's tails come out of people's foreheads and that kind of thing.

But it was Cor who worked himself hardest. Hour after hour, he sat by the lake with his black book practicing his monster-raising spell. He didn't eat, he scarcely slept, but he wouldn't stop. There was something special about the Monster of the Serpentine, only he couldn't remember what it was. There was a lot he couldn't remember these days, but he wasn't going to give up. There was nothing Cor wouldn't have done to bring back the Prince—unbopped and unsacked—to the parents who wanted him so much.

The only thing that still worried the rescuers was how to make Raymond Trottle come to the park. Of course it would be easy to call him by magic as Cor had called the ghosts, but they had promised faithfully not to use any magic directly on the Prince.

It was Ben who thought of what to do. "There's a boy at Raymond's school called Paul who's the son of a duke. Raymond would do anything to keep up with him. If we pretend that Paul's giving a secret party by the lake, I'm sure Raymond will come." Then his face became troubled. "Of course, it's cheating, I suppose. It's a lie."

But Cor was firm about this. "Bringing Raymond back to the Island is like a military campaign. Like a war. In a war, a soldier might have to tell a lie, but he'd still be serving his country."

Ben's plan worked. Melisande knew a siren who worked in Fortlands showing off the dresses, and she "borrowed" a posh invitation card, and Ben pretended that Paul had bribed him to deliver it.

And just before twelve o'clock on Midsummer's Eve, Raymond Trottle, in his jazziest clothes, arrived at the edge of the lake—and found a great throne which the trolls had built for him and a host of people who raised their arms and hailed him as a prince.

"A prince?" said Raymond. "Me?"

"Yes, Your Highness," said the Wizard, and told Raymond the story of his birth.

Raymond listened and, as he did so, a smug, self-satisfied smile spread across his face.

"I always knew I was special," he said. "I knew it"— and he climbed onto his throne.

CHAPTER 9

THERE HAD BEEN NOTHING like it for a hundred years.

The witches had made a circle of protection round the lake which no one could cross; everything inside it was invisible to any stray wanderers. Light came from the flaring torches of the wizards and from the glow-worms which Gurkie had coaxed into the trees—hundreds of them, glimmering and winking like stars. And there were real stars too: the night was clear, the moon shone down calmly on the revels.

"Doesn't it look *beautiful!*" whispered Ben. He hadn't expected to be allowed to watch, but Odge had told him not to be silly.

"Of course you're watching. We'll hide in the shrubbery with the mistmaker; no one will mind you being there."

And they didn't. It was strange how well Ben fit in. He spoke to the ghosts as easily as the Islanders, and even Odge's aunt, the Old Woman of Gloominess, had patted him on the head without turning him the least bit bald.

The Raymond Trottle Magic Show began with a flypast of Important Birds.

First a skein of geese flew in perfect formation across the moon, dipping their wings in salute as they passed over the Prince. Next the enchanter who had brought them called up a cloud of coal-black ravens who swooped and circled over Raymond's head—and then he stretched out an arm, and from a tree full of nightingales came music so glorious that Ben and Odge vanished for a moment as the mistmaker folded his paws over his chest and sighed.

Last came three dozen snow-white doves, which did the most amazing aerial acrobatics and turned to green, to orange, to pink, as the wizards changed the light on their flares. Then one bird left the flock, pulled a sprig of greenery from a laurel bush, flew with it in his beak to Raymond's throne—and laid it in his lap. It was just like this that the dove in the ark had come to Noah and shown him that his troubles were over, and all the watchers were very much moved.

And what did Raymond Trottle say? He said: "I've seen that on the telly."

But now the waters of the lake began to shimmer and shine. Then slowly, very slowly—three spouts of water rose from the center, and on the top of each spout sat a beautiful girl who began to sing and comb her hair.

"Of course, there are far more mermaids than this on the Island, Your Royal Highness," said Cor who was standing beside the Prince.

Not only more but of better quality, thought the wizard, who was beginning to realize what Ernie had meant when he said magic wasn't what it was. One of the mermaids came from the Pimlico Swimming Baths, and the chlorine in the water hadn't done much for her voice; the second had cut her hair into spikes after a pop group came to give an open-air concert by the lake where she lived, so though she could sing, she couldn't really comb. As for the third lady, she was Melisande from the fountain at Fortlands, and as she sang and combed, she kept pointing to her feet. No one knew why she minded so much about being taken for a mermaid, but she did.

Everyone clapped when it was over, though Raymond didn't seem very excited, and then Melisande's uncle, whom they called the Plodger, came forward. He was wearing his wellies and the woolly hat he wore to work in the sewers, but he bowed very respectfully to the Prince and said: "I shall search for the treasure of the lake."

He then walked to the water's edge . . . plodged into the shallows, kept on till the water came to his waist, his chin, his woolly hat . . . and disappeared!

No one was worried about this because merrows can breathe under water, but they were very interested.

The Plodger was gone a long time, and when he came back he was holding a large fish by the tail. The fish was flopping and wriggling, and the Plodger, though covered in slime and waterweed, looked pleased.

The wizards and witches whispered among themselves because they knew what was coming, and in the bushes Odge said: "This is going to be good; he's found a Special Carp!"

The Plodger came right up to Raymond; he still held the fish upside down, and the fish went on wriggling and thrashing its tail. Then suddenly it gave a big hiccup and out of its mouth there came—a beautiful ring! Swallowing rings is something certain fish do—one can read about it in the fairy tales—but finding a fish who has done it when you're wandering about on the bottom of a gray and murky lake is really difficult, and from the watchers there came another burst of clapping.

The Plodger then thanked the fish and threw him back into the lake, and Raymond looked at the ring.

"It isn't gold," he said. "It isn't a proper one. You couldn't get money for it in a shop."

Cor shook his head, and the merrow went off looking hurt. It was true that the ring had come out of a Christmas cracker, but what had that to do with anything? The special fish had trusted him; he had given up the ring that had been in his stomach for ten years—the ring that was part of his life as a fish—and all the Prince wanted to know was if he could sell it in a shop.

After that came the chorus of banshees. They'd had a busy week wailing in a football stadium because they knew that England was going to lose the European Championship, but they'd taken a lot of trouble, putting on their white shrouds and looking properly sinister and sad. And the songs were sinister and sad too—songs about darkness and dread and doom and decay.

When the banshees had finished, Raymond wanted to know if they were going to be sawn in half.

"There's always people sawn in half when there's magic on the telly," he said.

Needless to say, the banshees didn't stay around after that, and Hans came on to do some weight lifting.

The ogre had washed off his fernseed and looked truly splendid in his leather shorts and his embroidered braces and the kneesocks with the tassel on the side.

First he picked up a park bench, twirled it over his head, and put it down. Then he plucked out a concrete drinking fountain, balanced it on his nose—and put it back. And then he turned to the statue of Alderman Sir Harold Henfitter, which had been put up a month before. The alderman was cast in bronze and rested on a slab of marble, and even Hans had to pull and tug several times before he could free him from the ground.

But he did it. Then he counted to one . . . to two . . . to three . . . and threw the ten-ton alderman into the air!

Everyone waited. They waited and waited, but nothing happened. Nothing ever *would* happen—and that was the point, of course. The alderman had been thrown with such force that he would never come down again. Even now, Sir Harold Henfitter is going round and round somewhere in space and will go on doing so until the end of time.

It is not easy to believe what Raymond did after this amazing trick. He pointed with his fat finger at the giant's midriff. He giggled. And then he said: "A button's come off his braces!"

No one could believe their ears. Making personal remarks is rude at any time, but at a moment like this! It was true there had been a slight twang as the button went missing—but it was only on one side, and the ogre's leather shorts had hardly slipped at all.

Still, the show had to go on. The wizards did some tricks with the weather, making it rain on one side of the lake and snow on the other, and calling up a rumble of thunder with lightning following *afterward*—and then it was time for refreshments.

Gurkie was in charge of these, and instead of arranging for an ice-cream lady to come with her tray, she had laid on something very special. She ran to the big elm growing by the water and called to the glowworms to come so that the tree was lit as brightly as on a stage. Then she tapped the bark and spoke softly to the tree— and lo, every one of its branches began to bear fruit. There were peaches like golden moons; apples whose red skins glistened; pears as big as two fists put together.

"We beg Your Highness to refresh himself," said Gurkie.

Raymond got out of his throne and waddled over to the tree. Then he said: "I don't like fruit; it's got pips in it. I want a gobstopper."

Everyone lost heart a little after that. Cor didn't know what a gobstopper was; they hadn't had them when he lived Up Here, and even when the troll called Henry Prendergast drew one for him, he didn't feel like conjuring one up. There is very little magic done with gobstoppers anywhere in the world—and in the end a kind witch who worked as a school cook got on her bicycle and found an all-night garage that sold sweets and brought one for Raymond, who sucked it, moving it from cheek to bulging cheek all through the second part of the show.

This began with Odge's aunt and her sewing circle. There were seven of these Old Women of Gloominess, and though all of them were fierce and hairy, Odge's aunt was definitely the fiercest and the hairiest. The ladies struck each other with baldness; they made newts come out of each other's nostrils; they gave each other chicken pox . . . And in the bushes, Odge sighed.

"Do you think I'll ever be like that?" she asked.

"Of course you will," said Ben stoutly. "You've just got to get a little older."

Gurkie's tree spirits came next. To get a spirit to leave his tree is not easy, but Gurkie had such a way with her that one by one they all stepped out: the old, gnarled spirit of the oak; the tall, gray slightly snooty spirit of the ash; the wavery spirit of the willow . . . The dance they did was as ancient as Stonehenge—only three humans had been allowed to watch it in a thousand years—and Raymond Trottle sat there, moving his gobstopper from side to side—and yawned.

And now came Cor's big moment. He walked to the edge of the lake, and the wizards and the witches, the banshees and the trolls all held their breath.

The wizard closed his eyes. He waved his wand and spoke the monster-raising spell . . . and nothing happened. Once more he raised his wand, once more he said the spell . . .

Still nothing . . . Cor's shoulders sagged. He was too old. His power was gone. For the third and last time, the wizard drew on his strength and spoke the magic words. He had turned away, the watchers were shaking their heads—and then there appeared on the waters of the lake a kind of . . . shudder. The shudder was followed by a ripple . . . then a whole ring of ripples, and from the center of the ring there came . . . slowly, very slowly . . . a head.

It was a large head, and human—but unusual. The head was followed by a neck, and the neck was followed by shoulders and a chest, but what came after that was not a man's body, it was the body of a horse.

And everybody remembered what it was that was different about a nuckelavee.

It wasn't that it had a man's head and a horse's body. Animals that are partly people, and people that are partly animals, are two a penny where there is magic. No, what was unusual about the nuckelavee was that he didn't have any skin.

As the monster looked about him, wondering who had called him from the deep, they could see the blood rushing about inside his arteries and his windpipe taking in air. They could see the curving shape of his stomach as it churned the nuckel's food; even the creature's

heart, patiently pumping and pumping, was as clear as if they were seeing it through glass.

No one could take their eyes off him; they were entranced! To be able to see a living body in this way—to be allowed to study the marvelous working of the muscles and nerves and glands—was an honor they could hardly believe, and a young cousin of the troll called Henry Prendergast decided then and there to become a doctor.

Of course, they should have known what was to come. They should have known that Raymond Trottle would spoil this amazing and wonderful moment—a moment so special that none of them forgot it as long as they lived. They should have known that this boy with his bulging cheeks and piggy eyes would hurt and insult this awe-inspiring creature, and he did.

"Eeek!" said Raymond. "Ugh! It's disgusting; it's creepy. I don't like it!"

Well, that was that, of course. The nuckel sank—and from the onlookers there came a great groan, for they knew it would be a hundred years before the monster showed himself again and they could once more study this miracle of nature.

After that, there was nothing to do except get to the end. The troll called Henry Prendergast shape-shifted himself into a bank manager and a policeman, and the witches did a few interesting things with toads; and then everybody raised their torches and hailed Raymond as Prince of the Island—and it was done.

"Well, Your Highness," said Cor, but he spoke without any hope. "Now do you see what powerful forces you would rule over if you came to the Island? Will you come with us?"

Raymond shrugged. "Well, I dunno. I don't think I fancy it." And then, "You didn't make gold, did you? I thought all wizards could make gold. Can you make it?"

"Certainly we can make it, Your Highness. Any wizard worth his salt can make gold, but it isn't very interesting to watch."

"I don't believe you. I don't believe you can do it."

Cor turned and clapped his hands, and three wizards came to him at once.

"His Highness wishes us to make gold," he said wearily. "Find me some base metal—a bit of guttering from a drainpipe . . . an old bicycle wheel . . . anything."

The wizards vanished and came back with a load of junk metal which they laid on the ground close to Raymond. "Shall we do it, sir?" they asked because Cor was looking desperately tired. But the old wizard shook his head. "Just light the fire," he said.

When it was lit, he bent over it. He didn't even bother to get out his wand or to consult his book of spells. Making gold is something wizards learn to do in the nursery.

Raymond, who had hardly seemed interested when the mermaids sang from a water spout, or the nuckel rose from the deep, couldn't take his eyes from what Cornelius was doing.

The old bicycle wheel, the tin cans glowed . . . flared . . . the flames turned green, turned purple, turned red . . . Cor muttered. Then there was a small thud, and the center of the fire was filled with a mass of molten metal which glinted and glittered in the light of the flares.

"Is that it? Is that really gold?" asked Raymond.

"Yes, Your Highness," said Cor. He blew on the metal, cooled it, and handed it to Raymond.

"And if I come to the Island, can you make more of it? As much as I want?"

The wizard nodded. "Yes, Your Highness." He could have said that no one used gold on the Island—that they either swapped things or gave them away, but he didn't.

"Then I'll come," said Raymond Trottle.

CHAPTER 10

HURRY UP, BOY," said Mr. Fulton, giving Ben a push. "You've got the potatoes to bring in from the cellar still, and there's the brass strip to polish and the milk bottles to swill."

The butler was a tall, grim man who ruled with a rod of iron and never smiled.

"He's in a dream this morning," said Mrs. Flint. "I've had to tell him three times to wipe down the stove." Cooks are often fat and cheerful, but she was thin and cross and seemed to hate the food she prepared.

Only the housemaid, Rosita, gave Ben a kind glance. The boy looked thoroughly washed out, as though he hadn't slept.

Rosita was right. Ben had scarcely closed his eyes after he crept in from the park the night before. He was glad, of course, that Raymond had agreed to go with the rescuers; he *had* to be glad. Cor and Gurkie had been so relieved that their job was done, but as he dragged the heavy sack of potatoes up the cellar steps he felt as wretched as he had ever felt in his life.

In half an hour, Raymond would leave the house and never come back. On Monday morning, he went to the house of a Mrs. Frankenheimer, who gave him exercises to cure his flat feet and knock-knees. Mrs. Frankenheimer was very easy-going and wouldn't notice if he didn't turn up, and he was going to meet the rescuers at the corner of her street instead of going to school. Just about the time that Ben would be sitting in his classroom and opening his arithmetic book, Raymond would be stepping out onto the sands of the Secret Cove.

As he went to fetch his schoolbag, Ben's foot bumped against the cat tray under his bed. He had already almost house-trained the mistmaker even in the three days he had hidden him in his room. The animal was incredibly intelligent, and the realization that he would never see him again suddenly seemed more than he could bear.

Ben had accepted his life—the early-morning chores, the drudgery again when he came home at night, but that was before he had found people who really understood him and were his friends.

And he had quarreled with Odge.

"You're coming with us, of course," Odge had said. "You're coming to the Island."

And he'd said: "I can't, Odge."

The hag had been furious. "Of course you can. If you're worried about Raymond being such a pain, you needn't be, because if he isn't any better by the time he's grown up, I'll start a revolution and have his head chopped off; you can rely on that!"

"It isn't Raymond, Odge. I don't care about him. It's my grandmother. She took me in because I had nobody, and I can't leave her now she's ill. You must see that."

But Odge hadn't seen it. She'd stamped her feet and called him names, and even when Cor had agreed with Ben and said you had to stand by people who had helped you, she went off in a huff.

Well, it didn't matter now. He'd never see any of them again.

Ben usually liked school, but this morning the shabby old building with the high windows made him feel as though he was in a trap. And to make things worse, his usual teacher was ill and the student who took over was obviously terrified of kids. It would be uproar all morning, thought Ben—and he was right.

At break he didn't join his friends but went off on his own to a corner of the play-yard. You had to take one day at a time when things were bad, Nanny had said. "You can always take just one more step, Ben," she told him, but today it seemed as though the steps would lead down the grayest, dreariest road he could imagine.

There was a grating in the asphalt, covering a drain, and he crouched down beside it, wondering if the Plodger was somewhere nearby in his wellies . . . and that made him think of Melisande and the nuckel with his interesting face . . . Well, that was over, and forever. He'd never see magic again, not an ordinary boy like him.

For a moment, he wondered whether to change his mind. The gump was still open. The rescuers had trusted him; they had told him where it was. They hadn't told Raymond, but they'd told him. He closed his eyes and saw the three-masted sailing ship parting the waves . . . saw the green hump of the Island with its golden sands, and the sun shining on the roofs of the palace . . .

Then the picture vanished and there was another picture in its stead. An old woman lying in a high hospital bed, shrunken, ill, watching for him as he came down the ward.

The teacher blew her whistle. The children began to stream back into the building, but Ben still lingered.

Then he looked up. A small girl was coming across the road toward him. She wore an old-fashioned blazer;

her thick black hair was yanked into two pigtails, and she was scowling.

Ben scrambled to his feet. He tried to be sensible—he really tried—but a lump had come into his throat, and he stretched his hand through the bars like a prisoner.

"Oh, Odge," he said. "I am so *terribly* pleased to see you!"

Raymond had not kept his promise. He had not turned up at the corner of Mrs. Frankenheimer's street as he said he would. They had waited and waited, but he had not come.

"We should have known that the pig boy would double-cross us," said Odge. "The others are in an awful

state. Gurkie keeps saying if she'd been a fuath, it wouldn't have happened, which is perfectly ridiculous."

"What's a fuath?"

"Oh, some really vile swamp fairy with all sorts of nasty habits. And the giant keeps talking about bopping and sacking and how it was all his fault because he didn't—and the wizard looks about two hundred years old. He really loves the King and Queen."

"But where is Raymond, then?"

"Well, that's it; nobody knows. He's not in the house—the ghosts have haunted all over. Mrs. Trottle's gone as well—Ernie thinks that Raymond must have blabbed, and she's done a bunk with him. And it's serious, Ben. There are only five more days till the Closing. He's got to be found."

Ben drew himself up to his full height, and the hag thought how fearless he looked suddenly, how strong. "Don't worry, Odge. We'll find him; I absolutely know we will."

Ernie was right. Raymond had blabbed. When his mother came to wake him and told him to hurry or he'd be late for Mrs. Frankenheimer, Raymond yawned and said: "I don't have to go to Mrs. Frankenheimer again. Not ever."

Mrs. Trottle sat down on the edge of his bed, sending waves of Maneater over the coverlet, and put her pudgy hand on Raymond's forehead.

"Now, don't be difficult, sweetikins. You know Mrs. Frankenheimer is going to make your feet all beautiful—and you really can't miss school again. The headmaster was quite cross last week. Just think, if you were expelled and had to go to a common school with ordinary children."

Raymond stretched his arms behind his head and smirked. "I don't have to go to school again either. I'm never going to school anymore. I'm a prince."

"Well, of course, you're a prince to your Mummy, dear," said Mrs. Trottle, giving him a lipsticky kiss. "But—"

"Not that kind of prince; I'm really one. I'm going to go away and rule over hundreds of people on a secret island."

"Yes, dear," said Mrs. Trottle. "That's a very nice dream you've had, but now please get dressed."

"It's not a dream," said Raymond crossly. "They told me. The old man in the park. And the lady with the beetroot in her hat. I'm going to be a famous ruler and I don't have to do anything I don't want to ever again."

Mrs. Trottle went on tutting and taking no notice. Then as she picked up Raymond's jacket, which he had thrown on the floor, she noticed grass stains on it, and in his buttonhole, a spray of ivy. Her eyes narrowed.

"Raymond! What is the meaning of this? You've been out after I put you to bed!"

Raymond shrugged. "You can't tell me what to do

now," he said. "And Dad can't either because I'm a prince, and they're coming to show me the secret way back this morning."

Mrs. Trottle now became very alarmed. She hurried into Mr. Trottle's dressing room and said: "Landon, I think Raymond's in danger. People have been giving him drugs—dreadful drugs—to make him believe all sorts of things. It's a plot to kidnap him and hold us up to ransom, I'm sure of it."

"Nonsense," said Mr. Trottle, stepping into his trousers. "Who would want to kidnap Raymond?"

This was not a fatherly thing to say, but Mr. Trottle's mind was on the bank.

"Anyone who knows we're rich. I'm serious. They've persuaded him that he's a prince so as to lure him away."

"Well, he isn't, is he?" said Mr. Trottle.

"Landon, will you please listen to me. I'm very worried."

"Then why don't you contact the police?"

"Certainly not!" There were all sorts of reasons why Mrs. Trottle didn't want the police snooping around in Trottle Towers. Then suddenly: "I'm going to take Raymond away. I'm going into hiding. Now. This instant. You can stay here and change the locks and look out for anything sinister."

She wouldn't wait a minute longer. Mrs. Trottle was a stupid woman, but when it came to protecting her son, she could move like greased lightning. Taking no notice as Raymond sniveled and whined and said he was a prince, he really was, she packed a suitcase. Half an hour later, she and Raymond drove away in a taxi, and no one who worked in Trottle Towers knew where they had gone.

The search for Raymond went on all that day and well into the next.

Everyone helped. The Ghosts of the Gump got in touch with the ghosts in all the other railway stations and soon there wasn't a train which drew out of London without a spectre gliding down the carriages looking for a fat boy with a wobble in his walk and his even wobblier mother.

The mermaids and the water nymphs checked out the riverboats in case the Trottles meant to escape by sea. The enchanter's special pigeons flew the length and breadth of the land delivering notes to road workers and garage men who might have seen the Trottles' car —and the train spotter called Brian (the one who got between the buffers and the 9:15 from Peterborough) sat all day by the computer at Heathrow, checking the passenger lists, though electricity is about the worst thing that can happen to a spectre's ectoplasm.

Ben had not returned to school after Odge came for him. He'd asked the headmaster for the afternoon off, and because he'd looked so peaky when he first came, the head had agreed.

"Don't come back till you're properly well," he had said—and that was something he didn't say to a lot of children.

But though Ben searched Trottle Towers for clues and tried to get what he could out of the servants, he too drew a blank. Mr. Trottle had returned at lunchtime with a locksmith and told everyone that his wife and son would be away for a long time. And that was all that anybody could discover.

Ben's first thought was that Mrs. Trottle had taken Raymond to her home in Scotland, but one of the banshees, who came from Glasgow, telephoned the station master at Achnasheen, and he swore there was no sign of the Trottles.

"You'd notice them soon enough," he'd said, "with their posh kilts they've got no right to wear, and their bossy ways."

The rescuers had returned to the summer house which now became the headquarters of the search. They had bought some blankets, and a primus and kettle, and some folding chairs—and Hans had painted up the notice saying PRIVATE: NO ADMITTANCE which blocked the path. Fortunately the head keeper was on holiday so nobody disturbed them, but just to make sure, Gurkie had spoken to the bushes that grew so thick and tangled that anybody passing by could see nothing. She had planted out the beetroot from her hat because people did seem to stare rather, and to stop it being lonely she had made a vegetable patch from which huge leeks and lettuces erupted. And a pink begonia on the other side of the lake had made such a fuss because it wanted to be near her that she'd moved it so as to grow beside the wooden steps.

But even though she could feed everyone and make them comfortable, Gurkie still worried dreadfully and thought she should have been a fuath.

"No, you shouldn't, Gurkie," said Ben firmly. "You being a fuath, whatever that is, is a perfectly horrible idea and it wouldn't have helped at all."

Nor would he let the giant moan on because he hadn't bopped and sacked the Prince.

"Raymond'll be found, I'm absolutely sure of it," said Ben.

Ben was changing, thought Odge; he was becoming someone to rely on. She watched as he put down a bowl of milk for the mistmaker. The animal had taken to lurching after Ben wherever he went and making offended noises when he wasn't immediately scratched on the stomach or picked up and spoken to. There was going to be a fuss from the mistmaker when they had to go back and part from Ben, thought Odge, and she wondered whether she should kill Ben's grandmother.

Killing people was the sort of thing hags were meant to do, but it had not been allowed on the Island, and without any practice it was probably a bad idea.

But what mattered now was finding Raymond. All that afternoon, all the evening and well into the night, they searched and searched—the wizards and the witches, the ghosts and the banshees and the trolls . . . and as soon as day broke they began again—but it was beginning to look as though Raymond and his mother had vanished from the face of the earth.

CHAPTER 11

THE QUEEN LEANT OUT of her bedroom window. She leant out so far that she would have fallen but for a dwarf whom the King had put in charge of holding her feet. He had been holding her feet for days now because she did nothing except look out to sea and watch for the three-masted ship.

"Oh, where is it?" she said for the hundredth time. "Why doesn't it come?"

There were men all over the Island peering through

telescopes, the dolphins searched the seas, and the talking birds—the mynahs and the parrots—were never out of the air. The instant the ship was sighted, rockets would flare up, but the Queen went on watching, her long hair streaming over the sill, as though by doing so she could will her son to come to her.

But the dwarf now sighed—he was growing tired—and the Queen dragged herself away and went into the next room which she had prepared for the Prince. His old, white-curtained cradle still stood in the corner, but the palace carpenters had made him a beautiful bed of cedar wood and a carved desk and a bookcase because she knew without being told that the Prince would love to read. She hadn't made the room fussy, but the carpet, with its pattern of mythical beasts and flowers, had taken seven years to make—and there was a wide window seat so that he could sit and look out over the waters of the bay.

But would he ever sit there? Would she ever come in and see his bright head turn toward her?

The King, coming into the room, found her in tears again.

"Come, my dear," he said, putting his arms round her, "there are five days still for the rescuers to bring him back."

But the Queen wouldn't be comforted. "Let me go to the Secret Cove, at least," she begged. "Let me wait there for him."

The King shook his head. "What can you do there, my love? You would only fret and worry, and your people need you."

"I would be closer to him. I would be near."

The King said nothing. He was afraid of letting his wife go near the mouth of the gump. If she lost her head and went through it, he could lose her as he had lost his son.

"Try to have patience," he begged her. "Try to be brave."

The King and Queen were not the only people on the Island to worry and grow afraid. The schoolchildren had been given a holiday during the nine days of the opening, but they had decorated the school with flowers and hung up banners saying WELCOME TO THE PRINCE. Now the flowers were wilting, the banners hung limp after a shower of rain. The bakers who had baked huge, three-tiered cakes for the welcoming banquet began to prod them with skewers, wondering if they were going stale and they should start again. The housewives who had ironed their best dresses shook them out and ironed them all over again because they'd grown crumpled.

As for the nurses in the cave, they had ordered a crate of green bananas before the Opening so that the second the ship was sighted they could rip it open and help themselves to the firm, just-ripened fruit—but when no news came, they nailed it up again, and now they were back to wailing and eating burnt toast.

Then that night the square began to fill up with some very strange people.

There had been rumors, quite early on, of discontent in the north of the island. Not just the kind of grumbling you always get from people who have not been chosen for a job they are sure they could do. Not just Odge's sisters complaining because their baby sister had been chosen and not them. Not just grumpy giants saying, what do you expect, sending a milksop who yodels to bring back the Prince? No . . . this was more serious discontent, and from creatures that were to be reckoned with.

And that evening, the evening of the fourth day of the Opening, they came, these discontented people of the north. They came in droves, filling the grassy square in front of the palace, and turned their faces up to the windows, and waited . . .

Strange faces they were too: the blue-black faces of the neckies with their lopsided feet . . . the slavering-tongued sky yelpers, those airborne hellhounds with their saucer eyes and fiery tongues, and the squint-eyed faces of the harridans.

There were hags in the square who made Odge's sisters look like tinsel fairies; there was a bagworm as long as a railway carriage; there was even a brollachan—one of those shapeless blobs who crawl over the ground like cold jellies and can envelop anyone who gets in the way.

And there were the harpies! They had elbowed their way to the front, these monstrous women with the wings and claws of birds—and even the fiercest creatures who waited with them gave them a wide berth.

"Tell them to choose a spokesperson, and we will hear what they have to say," said the King.

But he knew why they had come and what they had to say, for these creatures of the North were as much his subjects as any ordinary schoolchild or tender-hearted fey. Not only that, they were useful. They were the police people. There was no prison on the Island—there was no need for one. No burglar would burgle twice if it meant a hellhound flying in through his window and taking pieces out of his behind. Any drunken youth going on the rampage soon sobered up after a squint-eyed harridan landed on his chest and squeezed his stomach so as to give him awful dreams—and you only had to say the word "harpy" to the most evil-minded crook and he went straight then and there.

And it was a harpy—the chief harpy—who pushed the others aside and came in to stand before the King.

She called herself Mrs. Smith, but she wasn't married and it would have been hard to think of anyone who would have wanted to sit up in bed beside her drinking tea. The harpy's face was that of a bossy lady politician, the kind that comes on the telly to tell you not to eat the things you like and to do something different with your money. Her brassy permed hair was strained back from her forehead and combed into tight curls, her beady eyes were set on either side of a nose you could have cut cheese with, and her mouth was puckered like a badly sewn buttonhole. A string of pearls was wound round her neck; a handbag dangled from her arm, and she wore a crimplene stretch top tucked into dark green bloomers with a frill round the bottom.

But from under the bloomers there came the long, scaly legs and frightful talons of a bird of prey, and growing out of her back, piercing the crimplene, was a pair of black wings which gave out a strange, rank smell.

"I have come about the Prince," said Mrs. Smith in a high, piercing voice. "I am disgusted by the way this rescue has been handled. Appalled. Shocked. All of us are."

Harpies have been around for hundreds of years. In the old days they were called the Snatchers because they snatched people's food away so that they starved to death, or fouled it to make it uneatable. And it wasn't just food they snatched in their dreadful claws; harpies were used as punishers, carrying people away to dreadful tortures in the underworld.

Mrs. Smith patted her hair and opened her handbag.

"No!" said the King and put up his hand. The handbags of harpies are too horrible to describe. Inside is their makeup—face powder, lipstick, scent . . . But what makeup! Their powder smells of the insides of slaugh-

tered animals, and one drop of their perfume can send a whole army reeling backward. "Not in the palace," he went on sternly.

Even Mrs. Smith obeyed the King. She shut her bag but once again began to complain.

"Obviously that feeble fey and wonky wizard have failed; one could hardly expect anything else. And frankly my patience is exhausted. Everyone's patience is exhausted. I insist that I am sent with my helpers to bring back the Prince."

"What makes you so sure that you can find him?" asked the King.

The harpy twiddled her pearls. "I have my methods," she said. "And I promise he won't escape us." She lifted one leg, opened her talons, covered in their sick-making black nail varnish, and closed them again—and the Queen buried her face in her hands. "As you see, my assistants are ready and waiting." She waved her arm in the direction of the window, and sure enough there were four more loathsome harpies, like vultures with handbags, standing in the light of the lamp. "I'll take a few of the dogs as well, and you'll see, the boy will be back in no time."

By "dogs" she meant the dreaded sky yelpers with their fiery breath and slavering jaws.

The Queen had turned white and fallen back in her chair. She thought of Gurkie with her gentle, loving ways . . . of Odge showing them the baby mistmaker she meant to give to the Prince . . . and old Cor, so proud to do this last service for the court. Why had they failed her? And how could she bear it if her son was snatched by bossy and evil-smelling women?

Yet how long could they still delay?

The King now spoke.

"We will wait for one more day," he said. "If the Prince has not been returned by midnight tomorrow, I will send for you all and choose new rescuers to find him. Till then everyone must return to their homes so that the Queen can sleep."

But when the Northerners had flown and slithered and hopped away, the King and Queen did anything but sleep. All night long, they stared at the darkness and thought with grief and longing and despair of their lost son.

CHAPTER 12

Mrs. Trottle was in the bath. It was an enormous bath shaped like a seashell. All round the edge of the tub were little cut-glass dishes to hold different kinds of soap and a gold-plated rack stretched across the water so that she could rest her box of chocolates on it, and her body lotions, and the sloppy love story she was reading. On the shelf above her head was a jar of pink bath crystals which smelled of roses, and a jar of green crystals which smelled of fern, and a jar of yellow crystals which smelled of lemon verbena, but the crystals she had put into the water were purple and smelled of violets. Mrs. Trottle's face was covered in a gunge of squashed strawberries which was supposed to make her look young again; three heated bath towels waited on the rail.

"Ta-ra-ra *boom*-de-ray!" sang Mrs. Trottle, lathering her round, pink stomach.

She felt very pleased with herself for she had foiled the kidnappers who were after her darling Raymond. She had outwitted the gang; they would never find her babykins now. They would expect her to go to Scotland or to France, but she had been too clever for them. The hiding place she had found was as safe as houses—and so comfortable!

Mrs. Trottle chose another chocolate and added more hot water with her magenta-painted toe. Next door she could hear the rattle of dice as Raymond played ludo with one of his bodyguards. She'd told Bruce that he had to let Raymond win, and he seemed to be doing what he was told. The poor little fellow always cried when he lost at ludo, and she was paying the guards enough.

Reaching for the long-handled brush, she began to scrub her back. Landon was staying at home to find out what he could about the kidnappers. They would probably go on watching the house, and once she knew who they were, she could hire some thugs to get rid of them.

That was the nice thing about being rich; there was nothing you couldn't do.

And that reminded her of Ben. She'd rung the hospital, and though they never told you what you wanted to know, it didn't look as though Nanny Brown was ever coming out again. The second the old woman was out of the way, she'd move against Ben. Thinking of Ramsden Hall up in the Midlands made her smile. They took only difficult children; children that needed breaking in. There'd be no nonsense there about Ben going on too long with his schooling. The second he was old enough, he'd be sent to work in a factory or a mine.

How she hated the boy! Why could he read years before Raymond? Why was he good at sport when her babykin found it so hard? And the way Ben had looked at her, when he was little, out of those big eyes. Well, she'd found a place where they'd put a stop to all that!

As for Raymond, she'd frightened him so thoroughly that there was no question of him wandering off again. He knew now that all the things he thought he'd seen in the park, and earlier in his bedroom, were due to the drugs he had been given.

"There's nothing people like that won't do to you if they get you in their clutches," she'd said to him. "Cut off your ear . . . chain you to the floor . . ."

She'd hated alarming her pussykin, but Raymond would obey her now.

What a splendid place this was, thought Mrs. Trottle,

dribbling soapy water over her thighs. Everything was provided. And yet . . . perhaps the violet bath crystals weren't quite strong enough? Perhaps she should add something of her own; something she had brought from home? Sitting up, she reached for the bottle of Man-eater on the bathroom stool. The man who mixed it for her had promised no one else had a scent like that.

"You're the only lady in the world, dear Mrs. Trottle, who smells like this," he'd said to her.

Upending the bottle, she poured the perfume gener-ously into the water. Yes, that was it! Now she felt like her true and proper self.

She leant back and reached for her book. The hero was just raining kisses on the heroine's crimson lips. Mr. Trottle never rained kisses on her lips; he never rained anything.

For another quarter of an hour, Mrs. Trottle lay hap-pily soaking and reading.

Then she pulled out the plug.

The Plodger liked his job. He didn't mind the smell of the sewage; it was a natural smell, nothing fancy about it, but it belonged. He liked the long dark tunnels, and the quiet, and the clever way the watercourses joined each other and branched out. He could tell exactly where he was—under which street or square or park—just from the way the pipes ran. It was a good feeling knowing he could walk along twenty feet under

Piccadilly Circus and not be bothered by the traffic and the hooting and the silly people trying to cross the road.

It wasn't a bad living either. It was amazing what people lost down the loo or the plughole of a bath, especially on a Saturday night. Not alligators—the stories about alligators in the sewers were mostly rubbish—but earrings or cigarette lighters or spectacles. His father had been in the same line of business, and his grandfather before him: flushers they were called, the people who made a living from the drains. Of course, having some fish blood helped—that's what merrows were, people who'd married things that lived in water. Not that there had been any tails in the family; merrows and mermen are *not* the same. Melisande was quite right to be proud of her feet; tails were a darned nuisance. No one could work the sewers with a tail.

Thinking about Melisande brought a frown to the Plodger's whiskery face. Melisande was all churned up. She'd got very fond of the fey—of all the rescuers—and now she worried because they couldn't find that dratted boy. All yesterday they'd searched, and they were at it again today, scuttling about Up There, but there wasn't any news.

Over his woolly hat the Plodger wore a helmet with a little light in it, and now, bending down, he saw a pink necklace bobbing in the muck. Not real—he could see that at once; plastic, but a pretty thing. It would fetch a few pence when it was cleaned up, and that was good enough for him; he wasn't greedy. Scooping it up in his long-handled net, he tramped on along the ledge beside the stream of sludge. He was near the Thames now, but he wouldn't go under it, not today. There were good pickings sometimes from the busy street that ran beside the river.

He turned right, plodded through a storm relief chamber, and made his way along one of the oldest tunnels close to Waterloo Bridge. You could tell how old it was with the brickwork being so neat and careful. No one made bricks like that nowadays.

Then suddenly he stopped and sniffed. His snout-like nose was wrinkled, his mouth was pursed up in disgust. Something different had just come down. Something horrid and yucky and *wrong*. Something that

didn't belong among the natural, wholesome smell of the drains.

"Ugh!" said the Plodger, and shook his head as though he could escape the sickly odor. A rat scuttled past him, and he fancied that it was running away from the gooey smell just as he wanted to do himself. Rats were sensible. You could trust them.

It wasn't just nasty—it was familiar. He'd smelled it before, that sweet, overpowering, clinging smell.

But where? He thought for a moment, standing on the ledge beside the slowly moving sludge. Yes, he remembered now. Not here—in quite a different part of the town.

He was excited now. Moving forward, he examined the inlet a few paces ahead. Yes; that was where it was coming from, running down in a slurp of bathwater. He tilted his head so as to shine the torch down the pipe, making sure he knew exactly where he was.

Then he turned back and hurried away, turning left, right . . . left again. A lipstick case bobbed up quite near him—brand new it looked too—but he wouldn't stop.

Half an hour later, he was lifting the manhole cover on the path between the Serpentine and the summer house inside the park.

No one, at first, could believe the wonderful news. They stood round the Plodger and stared at him with shining eyes.

"You really mean it? You've found the Prince?" asked Gurkie, holding a leek which had sprung out of the ground before she could stop it.

The Plodger nodded. "Leastways, I've found his mother."

"But how?" Cornelius was completely bewildered. Surely the Trottles weren't hiding in the sewer?

The Plodger answered with a single word.

"Maneater," he said.

"Maneater?" The wizard shook out his ear trumpet, sure he had misheard.

"That rubbishy scent Mrs. Trottle uses. It's got a kick like a mule. I used to smell it when I worked the drains under Trottle Towers. And just now I smelled it again."

The ring of faces stared at him, breathless with suspense.

"Where—oh, please tell us? Where?" begged Gurkie.

"I can tell you for certain," said the Plodger with quiet pride, "because I followed the outlet right back. It came from the Astor. That's where Mrs. Trottle's taken Raymond. She's holed up here in London, and in as clever a place as you can find. Getting the perisher out of there'll be like getting him out of Fort Knox."

The Astor was a hotel, but it was not an ordinary one. It was a super, luxury, five-star, incredibly grand hotel. The front of the hotel faced a wide street with elegant shops and nightclubs, and the back of the hotel looked out over the river Thames with its bridges and passing boats. Gentlemen were only allowed to have tea in the Astor lounge if they were wearing a tie, and the women who danced in the ballroom wore dresses which cost as much as a bus driver earned in a year. The Astor had its own swimming pool and gym and, in the entrance hall, were showcases with one crocodile-skin shoe in them, or a diamond bracelet, and there was a flower shop and a hairdresser and a beauty salon so that you never had to go outside at all.

Best of all was the famous Astor cake. This was not a real cake; not the kind you eat. It was a huge cake made out of plywood, painted pink and decorated with curly bits that looked like icing and every night while the guests were at dinner, it was wheeled into the restaurant, and a beautiful girl jumped out of it and danced!

Needless to say, ordinary people didn't stay in a hotel like that. It was pop stars and business tycoons and politicians and oil sheiks who came to the Astor, and people of that kind are usually afraid. Pop stars are afraid of fans who will rush up to them and tear their clothes, and politicians are afraid of being shot at by people they have bullied, and oil sheiks and business tycoons like to do their work in secret.

So the Astor had the best security service in the world. Guards with armbands and walkie-talkies

patrolled the corridors, there were burglar alarms everywhere and bomb-proof safes in the basement where the
visitors could keep their jewels. Best of all, there was a
special penthouse on the roof built of reinforced concrete, and the rooms in it had extra-thick walls and
secret numbers and lifts which came up inside them so
that they weren't used by the other guests at all. What's
more, the penthouse was built round a helicopter pad so
that these incredibly important people could fly in and
out of the hotel without being seen by anyone down in
the street.

And it was one of these secret rooms—Number 202
—which Mrs. Trottle had rented for herself and Raymond. Actually, it wasn't one room: it was a whole
apartment with a luxurious sitting room and a bedroom
with twin beds so that Mrs. Trottle could watch over
her babykin even when he slept. Even so, she had
checked into the hotel under a different name. She'd
called herself Lavinia Tarbuck, and Raymond was Ro-
land Tarbuck, and both of them wore dark glasses so
that they stumbled a lot but felt important.

Although the Astor bristled with security men,
Mrs. Trottle had hired two bodyguards specially for
Raymond. Bruce Trout was a fat man with a ponytail,
but the fatness wasn't wobbly like Raymond's; it was
solid like lard. His teeth had rotted years ago because he
never cleaned them and his false ones didn't fit, so they

weren't often in his mouth. They were usually behind the teapot or under the sofa. Not that it mattered. If there was trouble, Bruce could kill someone even without his teeth and had done so many times.

But it was the other bodyguard that was the most feared and famous one in London. Doreen Trout was Bruce's sister, but she couldn't have been more different. She was small and mousy with a bun of gray hair and weak blue eyes behind round spectacles. Doreen wore lumpy tweed skirts and thick stockings—and more than anything, she loved to knit. She knitted all day long: purple cardigans and pink booties and heather-mixture ankle socks . . . Clackety-click, clickety-clack went Doreen's needles from morning to night—and they were sharp, those needles. Incredibly sharp.

There are certain places in the human body which are not covered by bones, and someone who knows

exactly where these soft places are does not need to bother with a gun. A really sharp needle is much less messy and scarcely leaves a mark.

Bruce was costing Mrs. Trottle a hundred pounds a day, but for Soft Parts Doreen, as they called her, she had to pay double that.

Mrs. Trottle had made a good job of scaring Raymond. He believed her when she said that everything he'd seen in the park and in his bedroom had been due to dangerous drugs that the kidnappers had put into his food, and when she told him not to move a step without his bodyguards, he did what he was told.

Life in the Astor suited Raymond. He liked the silver trolley that came in with his breakfast, and the waiters calling him "sir," and he liked not having his father there. Mr. Trottle sometimes seemed to think that Raymond wasn't absolutely perfect, and this hurt his son. Best of all, Raymond Trottle liked not having to go to school.

Because the bodyguards were so careful, Mrs. Trottle soon allowed her son to leave his room. So he sat and giggled in the Jacuzzi beside the swimming pool, and went to the massage parlor with his mother, and bought endless boxes of chocolate from the shop in the entrance hall. In the afternoon, the Trottles ate cream cakes in the Palm Court Lounge, which had palm trees in tubs and a fountain, and at night (still followed by the bodyguards) they went to the restaurant for dinner and watched the girl come out of the Astor cake.

She was a truly beautiful girl, and the dance she did was called the Dance of the Seven Veils. When she first jumped out, she was completely covered in shimmering gold, but as she danced she dropped off her first veil . . . and then the next . . . and the next one and the next. When she was down to the last layer of cloth, all the lights went out—and when they came on again, both the girl and the cake had gone.

Raymond couldn't take his eyes off her. He thought he would marry a girl like that when he grew up, but when he said so to his mother, she told him not to be silly.

"Girls who come out of cakes are common," said Mrs. Trottle.

What she liked was the man who played the double bass. He had a soaring moustache and black soulful eyes, and he called himself Roderigo de Roque, but his real name was Neville Potts. Mr. Potts had a wife and five children whom he loved very much, but the hotel manager had told him that he must smile at the ladies sitting close by, so as to make them feel good, and so he did.

Mrs. Trottle liked him so much that on the second night she decided to go downstairs again after Raymond was in bed and listen to him play.

First though, she put a call through to her husband.

"Have you done what I told you? About Ben?"

"Yes." Mr. Trottle sounded tired. "Are you sure . . . ?"

"Yes, I'm perfectly sure," snapped Mrs. Trottle. "Tell the servants he may leave very suddenly, and I don't want any talk about it." She paused for a moment, tapping her fingers on the table and smiling as she thought of the neat plan she had made to get rid of the boy. "Remember, Ben is to be told *nothing*. What about the kidnappers? Any sign of them?"

"No."

"Well, go on watching," said Mrs. Trottle. Then she sprayed herself with Maneater and went downstairs to make eyes at Mr. Potts as he sawed away on his double bass and wished it was time to go home.

CHAPTER 13

ABSOLUTELY EVERYONE wanted to help in rescuing Raymond from the Astor. The ghosts wanted to, and so did the banshees and the troll called Henry Prendergast—and Melisande sent a message to say that she was moving into the fountain in the Astor so as to keep an eye on things.

But before they could make a plan to snatch the Prince, there was something they felt had to be done straightaway, and that was to send a message to the Island.

"They'll be getting so worried, the poor King and Queen," said Gurkie. "And even if everything goes smoothly, it could take another two days to get Raymond out. If they thought he was lost or hurt, it would break their hearts."

But how to do this? Ernie offered to go through the gump again and speak to the sailors in the Secret Cove, but Cor shook his head.

"Your poor ectoplasm has suffered enough," he said.

This was true. There is nothing worse for ectoplasm than traveling in a wind basket, and using ghosts as messengers is simply cruel.

Luck, however, was on their side. The nice witch who worked as a school cook and had fetched Raymond's gobstopper during the Magic Show, had decided to go through the gump immediately and make her home on the Island. She'd gone to work on Monday morning and been told she was being made redundant because the school had to save money, and she didn't think there was any point in hanging about Up Here without any work.

"I don't say as I like Raymond because I don't, but I dare say by the time he's on the throne I'll be under the sod," she said, coming to say good-bye.

Needless to say she was very happy to take a message to the sailors in the Secret Cove, so that problem was solved.

"Tell them there is nothing to worry about. The Prince is found and we hope to bring him very soon," said Cor, who actually thought there was quite a lot to worry about, such as how to get into the Astor, how to bop and sack the detestable boy, how to carry the wriggling creature to the gump. But he was determined not to upset the King and Queen.

So the witch, whose name was Mrs. Frampton, said she would certainly tell them that and made her way to King's Cross Station, and in no time at all she was stepping out onto the sands of the Secret Cove.

No one can be a school cook and work with children and be gloomy, and Mrs. Frampton was perhaps more cheerful than she needed to be. At all events, the message that a sailor (traveling like the wind in a pinnace) carried back to the Island, was so encouraging, that the Queen started to laugh once more and the schoolchildren put fresh flowers in the classroom and everyone rejoiced. Any day now, any hour, the Prince would come! The nurses opened the crate of bananas again— and most importantly, the harpies and the sky yelpers and all the other dark people of the North were told that they would not be needed; that the Prince was found and coming, and all was wonderfully well!

By the second day of watching Raymond, Bruce was thoroughly fed up. When you are a thug and used to being with gangsters, you aren't choosy, but he'd never met a boy who opened a whole box of chocolates and guzzled it in front of someone else without offering a single one. Bruce didn't like the way Raymond whined when he was being beaten at ludo, and he thought a boy sending up for someone to give him a massage when he hadn't taken any exercise was thoroughly weird.

All the same, Bruce did his job. He never let Raymond out of his sight, he kept his gun in its holster, he tasted the food that was sent up in case it was poisoned—and each morning he went into the bathroom as soon as Raymond woke so as to make sure there were no crazed drug fiends lurking behind the tub or in the toilet.

Now, though, he came out looking rather pale.

"There's something funny in there. It felt sort of cold, and the curtain moved, I'm sure of it."

Doreen Trout went on knitting. She knitted as soon as she woke. This morning it was a pair of baby's booties—very pretty, they were, in pink moss stitch, and the steel of the needles glinted in the sun.

"Rubbish," she said. "You're imagining things."

She got up and went into the bathroom. Her empty needle flashed. She waited. No screams followed, no blood oozed from behind the pierced curtains.

"You see," she said. "There's nobody there."

But she was wrong. Mrs. Partridge was there, and a nasty time she was having of it. She was a shy ghost and hated nakedness, but she had set herself to haunt the Trottles' sleeping quarters and get the layout, and though the sight of Mrs. Trottle in her underwear spraying Maneater into her armpits had made her feel really sick, she was determined to stick to her job.

Mrs. Partridge was not the only person watching the Trottles. Cor had decided that a day spent studying their movements was necessary before a proper plan to rescue Raymond could be made. So Ernie was floating through the kitchen quarters looking for the exits, peering at the switchboards which controlled the lights . . . The troll called Henry Prendergast, disguised as a waiter, loaded Raymond's breakfast trolley . . .

And there were others. Down in the laundry room, an immensely sad lady had gotten herself taken on as a temporary laundry maid and wept a little as she counted the sheets and studied the chute which sent the dirty washing down into the basement. She didn't cry because she was particularly troubled, but because she was a banshee, and weeping is what banshees do.

By ten-thirty, Raymond said he was bored.

"I want to go and buy something," he said.

So the Trottles went down in the lift with their bodyguards, and Raymond went into the gift shop in the hotel and grumbled.

"They haven't got the comic I want. And the toys are rubbish."

Mrs. Trottle went shopping too. She decided to buy a beautiful red rose to tuck into her bosom at dinner so that the double bass player would notice it and smile at her.

The flower shop though looked different today, and the lady who served in it seemed to be puzzled.

"Everything's taken off," she said. "Look at that rubber plant—I'll swear it's grown a foot in the night. And that wreath . . . it's twice the size it was."

The wreath was made of greenery and lilies. The hotel always kept wreaths because a lot of the people who stayed at the Astor were old and had friends who died.

Mrs. Trottle bent her head to smell a lily, wondering if the double bass player would prefer her with one of those—and jerked her head back. If it wasn't impossible, she'd have said that someone had pinched her nose.

Someone had. Flower fairies look much like they do in the pictures: very, very small with gauzy wings—but they are incredibly bad tempered because of people sticking their faces into the places where they live and *sniffing*. Seeing the hairy insides of someone's nostrils is not amusing, and though this particular fairy had offered to go to the Astor and help Gurkie, she certainly wasn't going to be *smelled*.

By lunchtime, the secret watchers were feeling thoroughly gloomy. It wasn't just that the bodyguards never let Raymond out of their sight, it was that Raymond himself was such a horrible boy. But it was Melisande who found out just what they were up against in rescuing him.

She had got her uncle to move her into the fountain in the Palm Court, and she was not having a nice time. This was because of the goldfish. In the Fortlands fountain she had been alone. Here she had to share with a dozen, droopy, goggle-eyed, fan-tailed goldfish who flapped their tails in her face and dirtied the water with their droppings and their food.

But Melisande was a trooper. She peeped out from under the leaves; she watched Raymond and Mrs. Trottle guzzle a slab of fudge cake not an hour after they had finished breakfast; she watched the daft way Mrs. Trottle leered at the double bass player when the orchestra played for the guests at tea.

And she watched as Doreen Trout came over to the fountain, sat down on the rim, and—with her eyes still fixed on Raymond—took out her knitting bag.

"Knit two, slip one," murmured Doreen.

Then she turned slightly—so slightly that Melisande hardly noticed it—and one of her needles plunged down into the water.

It was all over in a second, and then she got up and

went back to stand beside Raymond—but the fan-tailed
goldfish she had speared lay floating, belly up, between
the leaves while his life's blood, draining away, came
down on Melisande's shocked and bewildered head.

There was only one thing that cheered up the hidden watchers—and that was the cake!

The cake was beautiful! The way it came in, all pink
and glowing, from a door beside the orchestra, the balloons and streamers that came down on top of it . . . and
the lovely girl who burst out of it and danced, tossing
away her golden veils, while the band played music so
dreamy and romantic that it made you weep.

And it was the cake which gave Cor his idea.

All day the watchers had reported to him where he sat
in the summer house with his briefcase beside him, tak-

ing notes, making maps of the hotel and the street out-side—and thinking. Now he was ready to speak.

It was close on midnight and everyone had come to listen. The Plodger had brought Melisande, carrying her wrapped in a wet towel, and now she sat in the bird-bath looking worried because she felt no one knew quite how dreadful Doreen Trout could be. The ghosts hov-ered on the steps, the troll called Henry Prendergast lay back in a deck chair eating a leek which Gurkie had put into his hand. He did not care for leeks, but he cared for Gurkie and was doing his best with it. Ben had crept out of Trottle Towers, and he and Odge were crouched on the wooden floor watching the mistmaker. Among the banshees and the flower fairies were Odge's great aunt and a couple of ducks.

Cor's plan, like all good plans, was simple. They would use the moment when the girl in the cake finished her dance and the lights went out to capture the Prince.

"Hans will bop him—very, very carefully, of course, using only his little finger—and drop him into the cake as it is wheeled away. No one will think of looking for him there."

"But won't the girl in the cake get a shock when the Prince is thrown in on top of her? Won't she squeak?" asked Gurkie.

Cor shook his head. "No," he said. "Because the girl

in the cake won't be there. The girl in the cake will be somebody else." He looked at Gurkie from under his bushy brows. "The girl in the cake," said the wizard in a weighty voice, "will be—you!"

"Me!" Gurkie blushed a deep and rosy pink. She had always longed to come out of a cake—always—but when her mother was alive, it was no good even thinking about it. Gym mistresses who run about blowing whistles and shouting "Play Up and Play the Game" are not likely to let their daughters within miles of a cake. "You mean I'm to do that dance? The one with the Seven Veils? Oh, but suppose I was left standing in only my—" She didn't say the word "knickers"—she never *had* said it. Saying "knickers" was another thing her mother had not allowed.

"You won't be," said Cor. "The lights will go off before that, when you still have one veil on."

"You'll do it beautifully, Gurkie," said Ben. "They'll go mad for you." And everyone agreed.

"But after that?" said the troll. "How will you get the Prince out of the cake and away? Hans may be invisible, but Raymond won't be, if we're not allowed to use magic on him, and the cake only gets wheeled as far as the artists' dressing room."

Cor nodded. "But there are other things in the dressing room. Such as the instruments that the players in the orchestra use. Among them a large double-bass case."

He paused, and everyone looked at him expectantly, beginning to get the drift.

"As soon as the cake arrives in there, Hans will transfer the Prince into the case—and the double bass player will carry him out of the hotel by the service stairs where a van will be waiting."

"But surely he'll notice," said Ernie. "Raymond must weigh about five times as much as a double bass."

"Yes. But you see it won't be the real double bass player. It'll be Mr. Prendergast." He turned to the troll. "You shape-shifted yourself into a bank manager and a policeman. Surely you can manage a double bass player with a black moustache and a cowlick in the middle of his forehead?"

The troll nodded. "No problem," he said. "I got a good look at him tonight."

The other details were quickly settled. Since they still had over a thousand pounds in banknotes, they were sure they could pay the real girl in the cake to let Gurkie take her place. "And I shall call Mrs. Trottle away with a phone message just before the cake comes in," said Cor. "Odge will pretend to be the double bass player's little daughter and tell the doorman that her father has to come home early. As for you, Ben, you must wait on the fire escape and signal to the van driver as soon as Raymond is packed and ready, so that he can back up against the entrance. And then off we go, all of us, through the gump with a whole day to spare!"

Ben, when the jobs were given out, sighed with relief. He'd been afraid that they wouldn't let him help, and he wanted more than anything to be part of the team.

But he felt guilty too because he knew that Odge thought he was going with them to the island.

"This time you're coming!" said Odge. "You *have* to!"

And Ben had said nothing. It was no good arguing, but you had to do what was right, and leaving Nanny Brown alone, ill as she was, couldn't ever be right. Only he wouldn't let himself think what it would be like after the rescuers had gone. He wouldn't let himself think of anything except how to get Raymond Trottle out of the Astor and bring the King and Queen their long-lost son.

CHAPTER 14

NANNY BROWN moved her head restlessly on the pillow. She was worried stiff. Why had Larina Trottle phoned to ask how she was? Larina didn't care tuppence how she was, Nanny knew that. Surely she couldn't be planning to send Ben away already? In which case Ben ought to have the letter now . . . But what if the police came to the hospital to ask questions? Perhaps they'd pull her out of bed and take her to prison? Ben wouldn't like that; he felt things far too much.

And here he was now! As he sat down beside her and took her hand, she thought what a handsome boy he was turning out to be.

"You've had your hair cut."

Ben nodded. Gurkie had pruned his hair with her pruning shears. She'd offered to curl it too, like she curled the petals of a rose, but Ben didn't think Nanny would like him with curly hair. Thinking of the rescuers made him smile—they were all so excited about tonight and getting Raymond out. Then he looked more closely at Nanny and his heart gave a lurch. She was nothing but skin and bone.

"Does it hurt you, Nanny? Are you in pain?"

"No, of course not," she lied. They'd offered her

some stuff to take away the pain, but she'd never let them dope her when Ben came. "What about Mrs. Trottle? How's she been?"

"She's still away—and Raymond, too."

Nanny nodded. That was all right, then. If Larina was away, she couldn't harm Ben, so the letter could wait. The nurses had promised faithfully to give it to Ben when the time came.

"And the servants?"

"They've been all right. They seem to let me do what I like, almost." But he was puzzled. The servants were almost *too* nice, and Mr. Fulton gave him an odd look now and again, as though he knew something. It made Ben uncomfortable, but he wasn't going to worry Nanny Brown.

And Nanny wasn't going to worry Ben about the nonsense the young doctor had come up with that morning. She knew her time was up, and she certainly didn't mean to go up to heaven stuck full of tubes.

But as Ben left the ward, he found the nice nurse, Celeste, waiting for him.

"Sister'd like a word with you, Ben," she said. "Would you come along to her room?"

The Sister had dark hair and kind eyes. "Ben, you're very young but you're a sensible boy, and there doesn't seem to be anyone else."

Ben waited.

"You're the next of kin, dear, aren't you? I mean, you're the only relation Mrs. Brown has?"

"Yes. I'm her grandson."

The nurse sighed and stabbed her pencil onto a notepad.

"You see, Ben, the doctors are thinking of operating on your grandmother. It would be a shock to her system and cause her some pain, but it might give her a bit longer."

Ben bit his lip. "When would that be?"

"The day after tomorrow. We thought you should know."

The day after tomorrow. The last day of the Opening. It would be all over then and the rescuers gone. Well, if he'd had any doubts, that settled it. To let her go through an operation by herself was not to be thought of.

"I'd like to be there when she comes round," he said. "I'd like to be with her."

"I'll ask the doctor," said the Sister—and smiled at him.

CHAPTER 15

MRS. TROTTLE had got the table she wanted—on the left of the band, which was where the cake came in and really close to the double bass player. She was sure he fancied her; every so often when he wasn't sawing away with his bow, his eyes seemed to meet hers. What a lovely player he was, and what a lovely man!

Raymond was sitting opposite, dressed to kill in a new silk shirt and spotty bow tie, and as she leant forward to wipe the dribble of cream from his chin, Mrs.

Trottle thought there wasn't a better-looking boy in the world. Her husband said she spoiled him, but Mr. Trottle didn't understand Raymond. The boy was sensitive. He *felt* things.

Bruce was standing by the far wall, his eye on Raymond. He was hungry, but no one thought of sending anything over for him to eat. His sister Doreen sat on a chair by the big double doors. Ordinary guests would have been surprised to see a woman knitting all through dinner, but there were enough people there who had used bodyguards in their time, and it gave them a good feeling to know that Soft Parts Doreen was in the room. No terrorists or assassins would get far with her around!

In the phone box across the street from the hotel, Cor was reading the instructions. Or trying to, but his spectacles kept falling off the end of his nose, and he didn't like the look of all those buttons.

"Insert money," mumbled the wizard. "Dial number . . ." But when he dialed it, something gloomy flashed onto the little gray screen and everything went dead. He tried again and the same thing happened. Then suddenly he lost patience. They weren't supposed to use magic on the Prince, but a telephone was different. He spoke the number of the Astor; he turned to the East, he uttered the Calling Spell—and on the reception desk of the hotel, the phone began to ring.

"Oh no! I can't come now." Mrs. Trottle glared at the page who had come to say that she was wanted on the telephone. The double bass player was playing something so dreamy that he must surely be playing it for her alone, and she almost decided to pluck the rose from her chest and throw it at him.

"The gentleman said it was very urgent, Madam," said the page—and Mrs. Trottle got up sulkily and followed him, while Bruce moved closer to Raymond and Doreen shifted slightly in her chair.

Hans now entered the room. He had been incredibly brave and offered to have fernseed even in his eye so that he could be completely invisible and still see where he was going. His little finger was stretched out ready to bop Raymond, and it trembled because the ogre was very much afraid. Suppose he bopped too hard and brought the Prince to the Island with a broken skull? On the other hand, suppose he didn't hit him hard enough so that he squealed when he was thrown into the cake?

If Hans was nervous, poor Gurkie was terrified.

"Oh Mother, forgive me," she muttered. She had been to Fortlands and bought some of the stuff they used for blackout curtains to make the last veil—the one she wore over her underclothes—and the underwear itself was bottle-green Chilprufe because her mother had always told her that it was what you wore next to the skin that mattered, so even if the lights didn't go out at exactly the right time, she would still be decent. All the same, as she stepped into the cake, Gurkie's teeth were chattering. At least the girl who usually did the Dance of the Seven Veils was happy! She'd grabbed the money Cor had given her and even now was going up in a jumbo on the way to sunny Spain.

"Ready?" asked the porter, coming to wheel her in.

"Ready!" squeaked Gurkie, from inside the layers of tissue.

The orchestra burst into a fanfare; balloons and streamers came down from the ceiling—and Gurkie burst out of the cake and began to dance.

Raymond didn't recognize her because even her face was veiled, and the light was rosy and dim, but everyone felt that something beautiful was going to happen, and they were right. Feys have always loved dancing—they dance round the meadows in the early morning, they twirl and whirl on the edge of the sea, and of all the twirlers and whirlers on the Island, Gurkie was the best. She forgot that her mother would have turned in her grave to see her in the dining room of the Astor Hotel like any chorus girl, she forgot that any minute Raymond Trottle would land with a thump on top of her. And as she danced, the orchestra followed the way she moved . . . got slower when she went slowly and quicker when she went fast, and there wasn't a single person in the dining room who could bear to take his eyes off her.

Gurkie dropped the first of her seven veils on the floor. She was thinking of all the lovely things that grew on the Island and of her cucumbers and how she would soon be home, but the people watching her did not know that. They thought she was thinking of them.

And Hans had reached Raymond's table. He was standing in the space left by Mrs. Trottle. He was ready.

The sixth veil dropped. The music got even soupier. Now as she danced, Gurkie was strewing herbs into the room, the sweet-smelling herbs she had brought in her basket to make people sleepy, to make them forget their troubles.

By the back entrance, Odge Gribble was explaining to the porter that her father had to leave early.

"My Mummy isn't well," she said with a lisp—and he nodded and pinched her cheek.

In the lavatory which led out of the dressing room, the troll waited. He looked so like the double bass player that his own mother wouldn't have known him. Ben, crouching on top of the fire escape, kept his eyes on the waiting van.

Back in the dining room, Gurkie dropped her fifth veil . . . her fourth . . . She still spun and whirled, but more slowly now—and the lights were turning mauve . . . then blue.

"Coo!" said Raymond Trottle as she danced past his table.

The third veil now . . . the second. And now Gurkie did begin to worry. What if the lights didn't go out? Was her last veil *really* thick enough?

But it was all right. Hans's little finger was stretched out over Raymond's head.

The orchestra went into its special swirly bit. The lights went out.

And at that moment, Hans bopped!

The getaway van was parked in the narrow road which ran between the back of the Astor and the river. It had been dark for some time; the passing boats had lit their lamps, and light streamed from the windows of the hotel.

The inside of the van was piled with blankets so that the Prince could be made comfortable on the way to the gump. All the rescuers' belongings were there because they were driving straight to the station.

And Odge's suitcase was there, carefully laid flat. The door of the van was open, and plenty of fresh air reached the mistmaker through the holes that Odge had drilled in it, so he should have been content, but he was not. He was too old for suitcases; he was a free spirit; he was used now to being part of things!

Rustling about in the hay, complaining in little whimpers, he put his sharp front teeth against the fiber of the case and found a weak place where the rim round one of the holes had frayed. Getting interested, beginning to see hope, he began to gnaw.

The driver noticed nothing. He had his eyes fixed on the boy who crouched on top of the fire escape. As soon as Ben signaled with his torch, he'd back up against the entrance.

In the dining room of the Astor, the guests waited for the cake; the orchestra played a tango.

"It's awfully hot in here," complained a girl at one of the tables, and called a waiter.

The mistmaker went on gnawing. He was pleased. Something was happening. The hole was getting bigger . . . and bigger . . . and bigger still. His whiskers were already through, and his nose . . .

Then quite suddenly he was free!

Trembling with excitement, he sat up on his haunches and looked about him. And at that moment, one of the waiters opened a window in the dining room, sending the sound of the orchestra out into the night.

Music! And what music! The mistmaker had never heard a full orchestra in his life. His eyes grew huge, his moustache quivered. Then with a bound he leapt out of the van and set off.

The driver's eyes were still on Ben.

Lolloping along like a lovesick pillow, the mistmaker crossed the road, leapt onto the bottom rung of the fire escape, missed . . . tried again. Now he was on and climbing steadily.

"Oom-pa-pa, oom-pa-pa," went the band. The violins soared, the saxophones throbbed . . .

Ben peered down the iron stairs, wondering if he had seen something white crossing the road. No, he must have been mistaken . . .

The Astor was beside the river, and the riverbank

was full of rats. Large, intelligent rats who had dug paths for themselves into the hotel. Panting up the first rung of the fire escape, the mistmaker found a hole in the brick and plunged into it. It came out near the kitchens, behind a store cupboard, and from there another rat-run led into the pantry where the waiters set out the trays to carry into the dining room. He only had to cross a passage, run through an open door . . .

And now he was where he wanted to be—where he absolutely had to be, facing that wonderful sound! He had arrived just as the cake was wheeled away and the room was in darkness, but that didn't matter because the band was still playing and it was a Viennese waltz!

The mistmaker made his way into the middle of the room and sat down. Never, never had he heard anything so beautiful! The fur on the back of his neck lifted; he shivered with happiness; his earlobes throbbed.

"Aaah!" sighed the mistmaker. "Aaah . . . aaah!"

The waves of mist were slight to begin with; he was puffed from the climb and he was overwhelmed. But as the beauty of the music sank deeper and deeper into his soul, so did the clouds of whiteness that came from him.

At one of the tables, an old gentleman began to cough. An angry lady leant across her husband and told the man at the next table to stop smoking.

"I'm not smoking," the man said crossly.

But as the lights came on again, the guests could see

that something odd was happening. The room was covered in a thick white mist—so thick that the Trottles' table could hardly be seen.

"It's smoke!" The room's full of smoke," shouted a girl in a glittery dress.

"No it isn't. It's tear gas!" yelled a bald man and put his napkin to his face.

"It's a terrorist bomb!" cried a fat lady.

Bruce was blundering round Raymond's chair, feeling for the boy. Perhaps he was hiding under the table, trying to get away from the creeping gas? Clutching his gun, he dived under the cloth.

The mistmaker was upset by the ugly shrieking. He moved closer to the band which was still playing. A good orchestra will play through thick and thin.

Once more he gave himself up to the beauty of the music; once more he sighed. But he was getting thinner now; he was no longer pillow-shaped. The whiteness that came from him was not so thick, and in a break in the mist, a woman in a trouser suit stood up and pointed: "Look! It's coming from that horrible thing!" she screeched.

"It's a poisonous rat! It's a rodent from outer space!"

"It's got the plague! They do that; they give off fumes and then they go mad and bite you!"

The cries came from all over the room. A waiter rushed in with a fire extinguisher and squirted foam all over a group of Arabs in their splendid robes. One of the Astor's own guards had seized a walking stick and was banging it on the floor.

And now something happened which put the mist-maker's life in mortal danger. The band gave up. The music stopped . . . and with it, the supply of mist which had helped to hide and shelter him. Suddenly cut off from the glorious sound, the little animal blinked and tried to come back to the real world. Then he began to run hither and thither, looking for the way back.

And Doreen Trout reached for her knitting bag.

In the artists' dressing room, Gurkie had climbed out of the cake. She had a bruise on her shoulder where Raymond's chin had hit her, but she was being brave. The Prince looked crumpled, but his breathing was steady. Only a few minutes now and he'd be stretched out in the van where she could make him comfortable.

"I bopped well?" asked Hans who had followed her into the dressing room.

"You bopped beautifully," said Gurkie.

The troll came out of the toilet and opened the double bass case.

"I'll take the feet," he said, and Hans nodded and went to Raymond's shoulders.

Everything was going according to plan.

It was at that moment that the door to the fire

escape burst open and Ben, ashen-faced and frantic, rushed into the room.

"The mistmaker's escaped," he said. "He's in the dining room. And they're going mad in there. They'll kill him."

"No!" Hans let go of Raymond, who fell back into the cake. "Our duty is to the Prince. You must not go!"

Ben did not even hear him. Before the ogre could move to stop him, he had reached the other door and was gone.

In the dining room, everyone was shrieking and joining in the hunt for the dangerous rodent from outer space. The Arabs whose robes had been squirted with foam were yelling at the waiter; a lady had fainted and fallen into her apple pie.

"There he is!" screamed a woman. "Behind the trolley!" And Bruce aimed, fired—and hit a bottle of champagne, which exploded into smithereens.

The mistmaker was terrified now. The shrieks and thumps beat on his ears like hammer blows; his head was spinning and he ran in circles, trying to find the way out.

"He's got rabies!" yelled a fat woman. "That's how you tell, when they go round and round like that."

"If he bites you, you're finished," shouted a red-faced man. "Get on a table; he'll go for your ankles."

The fat lady did just that, and the table broke, sending her crashing to the ground. "Don't let him get me!" she screamed. "Squash him! Finish him!"

Bruce had seized a chair and was holding it above his head as he stalked the desperate little beast. Now he brought it down with a thump, and one leg came off and rolled away.

"He's missed," moaned the woman on the floor.

Once again Bruce raised the chair, once again he brought it down, and once again he missed.

Doreen Trout had not screamed. She had not thumped. She had not picked up heavy chairs or reached for her gun. All she had done was take out her favorite knitting needle. It was a sock needle of the finest steel and sharper than any rapier. She had judged its length, and it would skewer the animal neatly without any waste.

"Get out of the way, oaf," she hissed at her brother. "I'm dealing with this. Just corner him."

This was easier said than done. The mistmaker, caught in the nightmare, scuttled between the tables, vanished into patches of whiteness, skittered on the foam. But his enemies were gathering. The saxophone player had jumped down from the bandstand and shooed him against the wall; a waiter with a broom handle blocked him as he tried to dive behind the curtains.

And now he was cornered. His eyes huge with fear, he sat trembling and waited for what was to come.

"Stand back!" said Doreen to the crowd—and began to move slowly toward the terrified animal. "Come on, my pretty," she cooed. "Come to your Mummy. Come and see what I've got for you."

The room fell silent. Everyone was watching Doreen Trout, holding her needle as she moved closer, and all the time talking in a coaxing, wheedling voice.

The mistmaker's whiskers twitched. He blinked; the delicate ears became flushed. Here was a low voice; a kind voice. He turned his head this way and that, listening.

"I've got lovely things for you in my bag. Carrots . . . lettuce . . ."

More than anything, the desperate creature wanted kindness. Should he risk it? He took a few steps toward her . . . paused . . . sat up on his haunches. Then suddenly he made up his mind, and in a movement of trust he turned over on his back with his paws in the air as he had done so often when he was playing with Ben and Odge. He knew what came next—that moment when

they scratched him so soothingly and deliciously all down his front.

Soft Parts Doreen looked down at the rounded, unprotected stomach of the little beast; at the pink skin still showing where his grown-up fur had not yet come.

Then she smiled and raised her arm.

The next second she lay sprawled on the floor. A boy had come from nowhere and leapt at her, fastening his arms round her throat.

"You murderess! I'll kill you; I'll kill you if you harm him!" shouted Ben.

The attack was so sudden that Doreen dropped her needle, which quivered, point down, in the carpet. Scratching and spitting, she tried to shake Ben off while her free hand crawled like a spider toward the embedded needle.

"Get the boy, idiot!" she spluttered at Bruce.

But that was easier said than done.

Every time it looked as though he could get a shot at Ben, some bit of Doreen got in the way. Anyway, his sister was sure to win—the boy fought like a maniac, but he was half her size, and her hand was almost on the needle. Now she was clawing at his face, and as he pushed her away and tried to free himself, his arm was clear of Doreen's body. Blowing a hole in the boy's arm was better than nothing, and carefully Bruce lifted his gun and aimed.

The next second he staggered back, reeling, while pieces of splintered wood rained down on his shoulders. The double bass player had gone mad and hit him on the head with his instrument.

Except that the real double bass player was up on the bandstand with his hand to his mouth staring down at the man who seemed to be him.

But Doreen's crawling fingers had reached the needle, pulled it out. Holding the glittering steel above Ben's throat, she brought it down in a single, violent thrust—just as Ben, with a superhuman effort, rolled out of her grasp.

"Ow! Help! Gawd!"

Bruce clutched his foot, hopped, tried to pull the needle out of his shoe. Maddened by pain, half stunned by the blow the troll had given him, he seized a brass table lamp.

Ben had turned, trying to catch the mistmaker. He had no time to dodge, no time to save himself. The base of the heavy lamp came down on his skull in a single crushing blow—and as the blood gushed from the wound, he fell unconscious to the ground.

"He's dead!" screamed a woman.

"I hope so," said Doreen softly. "But if not . . ."

She pulled the needle out of her brother's shoe and knelt down beside Ben, searching for the soft hollow beneath his ear.

But then something terrifying happened. As she bent over the boy, she was suddenly pushed back as if by an invisible hand—pushed back so hard that she fell against the plate-glass window, which broke with a crash.

It was incredible but they could all see it—slowly, gently, the wounded boy rose into the air. . . . Higher he rose, and higher . . . Blood still trickled from his scalp, he lay with one arm dangling and his head thrown back . . . lay *in the air*, unsupported and clearly visible above the mist.

"He's going to heaven!" cried someone.

"He's been called up to Paradise!"

And that was how it looked to everyone there. They had seen pictures of saints and martyrs who could do that . . . levitate or lift themselves up and lie there in the clouds.

But that wasn't the end of it. Now the boy who *had* to be dead began to float slowly, gently, away, high over everyone's head . . . until he vanished through the door.

CHAPTER 16

O N THE MORNING of the eighth day of the Opening, the Royal Yacht set off from the Island, bound for the Secret Cove.

Not only was the Queen aboard, but the King and several of his courtiers, for he understood now that the Queen had to get as close as she could to the place where the Prince would appear—if he appeared at all. Two days had passed since the cheerful message from the witch, and still there was no sign of their son. All along the King had tried to comfort his wife, but now even he was finding it hard to be brave.

Down below, a special cabin had been prepared for the Wailing Nurses. They had begged to be allowed to come along, but since they hadn't washed for nine years they had to be kept well away from the other passengers. With them had come a new crate of bananas because the first batch had become overripe, and the Queen had managed a smile as she saw it carried aboard because it meant the triplets, at least, still hoped.

As the Royal Yacht drew out of the harbor, a second and much larger boat pulled up its anchors, ready to follow. This was a ship chartered by people on the Island who could not fit onto the King's yacht but who also wanted to be there for the last day of the Opening. Most of these were people who cared very much about the little Prince and longed and longed for him to be brought back safely, even now at the eleventh hour. But some—just a few—were peevish grumblers: people who wanted to gloat over the old wizard and the loopy fey and the conceited little hag when they came back in disgrace. And there were some—there are always such people even in the most beautiful and best-ruled places —who just wanted an outing and a chance to gawp at whatever was going to happen, whether it was good or bad.

The Royal Yacht skimmed over the waves. The charter boat followed more slowly. In their cabin the nurses wailed and tried to think of ways of punishing themselves, but not for long because they became seasick and no one can think of a worse punishment than that.

The Queen would not go below. She stood leaning over the rails, her long hair whipped by the wind, and over and over again she said: "Dear God, please let him come. Please let him come. I will never do anything bad again if only you let him come."

Poor Queen. She never *had* done anything bad; she was not that sort of person.

They had been at sea for only a short time when something happened. The sky darkened; a black thundercloud moved in from the west, and a few drops of rain fell on the deck.

Or was it rain?

The sailors who had been below hurried up the ladders, preparing for a storm. The gulls flew off with cries of alarm; the dolphins dived.

It was not a storm, though, and the swirling blackness was not a cloud. The sky yelpers came first: a pack of baying, saucer-eyed dogs racing overhead, dropping their spittle on the deck where it hissed and sizzled and broke into little tongues of flame which the sailors stamped out.

But it was the harpies which made the Queen sway and the King run to her side.

They flew in formation like geese, with Mrs. Smith at their head and the others in a V shape behind her: Miss Green, Miss Brown, Miss Jones, and Miss Witherspoon. Their handbags dangled from their arms; their varnished talons hung down from their crimplene bloomers . . . and their unspeakable stench beat against the clean, salty air of the sea.

From the charter ship, a cheer went up. These were the real rescuers, the proper ones. And about time too! The King and Queen had waited till the last possible moment before sending in these frightful women, and there were those who thought they had delayed too long.

The harpies flew on, the dogs racing before them. In an hour they would be through the gump. The Queen's knuckles whitened on the rail, but she would not faint; she would bear it.

"There was nothing to do, my dear; you know that," said the King.

The Queen nodded. She did know it. There were twenty-four hours left; only one day. These ghastly creatures were her only hope.

CHAPTER 17

B EN LAY ON THE FLOOR of the summer house, his head pillowed on the wizard's rolled-up cloak. His eyes were closed; his face, in the light of the candles, was deathly pale. Since Hans had carried him out of the Astor, he had not stirred.

Gurkie sat beside him, holding his hand. She had rubbed healing ointment into his scalp; the bleeding had stopped, the wound was closing—but the deeper hurt, the damage to his brain, was beyond her power to heal. And if he never came round again . . . if he lived forever in a coma . . . or if he died . . .

But no one could bear to think of that. Cor sat still as stone in the folding chair. He was shivering, but they hadn't been able to stop him giving his cloak to Ben.

"I am too old," he thought. "I have failed in my mission and brought harm to as brave a child as I shall ever see."

Hans was crouched on the steps. His fernseed had gone blotchy, and every so often a moan escaped him. "Oi," murmured the giant. "Oi." If he had followed Ben at once into the dining room instead of waiting by the Prince, he could have prevented this dreadful accident, and he knew that he would never forgive himself.

The manhole cover on the path now lifted slowly, and the Plodger climbed out, still in his working clothes.

"Any news?" he asked. "Has he come round?"

The wizard shook his head, and the Plodger sighed and made his way back into the sewer. Melisande was going to be dreadfully upset.

It was well past midnight. In Trottle Towers the servants slept, believing that Ben had already been taken to his new "home." The ghosts had come to stand round Ben as he lay unstirring and then had gone back to the guarding of the gump.

It was amazing how many people had come to ask

after Ben, people who should scarcely have known the boy. Wizards and witches, the banshee who had worked in the laundry room of the Astor . . . the flower fairy who had pinched Mrs. Trottle on the nose. It was extraordinary how many people cared.

It was the last day of the Opening. They had expected to be back on the Island by now, but no one even thought of leaving. Ben had helped them from the first moment they had seen him cleaning shoes in the basement of Trottle Towers; he had seemed at once to belong to them. Not one of the rescuers dreamt of abandoning him.

Odge was not with the others as they clustered round Ben. She had gone off by herself and was sitting by the edge of the lake, wrapped in her long black hair.

Ben was going to die; Odge was sure of it.

"And it's my fault," she said aloud. "I brought the mistmaker, and it was because he went to save him that Ben was hurt."

The mistmaker lay beside Ben now; Odge had been able to snatch him up when the ogre brought Ben out of the dining room. If Ben woke, he would see the little animal at once and know that he was all right, but he wouldn't wake. No one could lie there so white and still and not be at death's door.

And if Ben died, nothing would go right ever again. She could grow an extra toe—she could grow a whole *crop* of extra toes—she could learn to cough frogs, and none of it would be any use. Only yesterday her great-aunt had taught her the Striking People with Baldness Spell, but what did that matter now? Hags don't cry—Odge knew that—but nothing now could stop her tears.

Then suddenly she lifted her head. Something had happened—something horrible! An evil stench spread slowly over the grass and crept through the branches of the trees. . . . The roosting birds flew upward with cries of alarm. A cloud passed over the moon. Running back to warn the others, she saw that they had risen to their feet and were staring at the sky.

The smell grew worse. A mouse in the bushes squealed in terror; a needle of ice pierced the warmth of the summer night.

And then she came! Her rancid wings fluttered once . . . twice . . . and were folded as she came in to land. Her handbag dangled from her arm; the frill round the bottom of her bloomers, hugging her scaly legs, was like the ruff on a poisonous lizard.

"Well, well," sneered Mrs. Smith. "Quite a cozy little family party, I see." She opened her handbag to take out her powder puff—and the rescuers fell back. The smell of a harpy's face powder is one of the most dreaded smells in the world. "One might think that people who have fallen down on their job so completely would at least show some signs of being sorry."

No one spoke. The nail polish on the harpy's ghastly talons, the loathsome hairspray on her permed hair, were making them feel dizzy and sick.

"Candles! Flowers! Giants in embroidered braces! Pshaw!" said Mrs. Smith. She put her claws on Gurkie's begonia and tore it out of the ground. "Well, you know why I'm here. To tell you you're finished. Demoted. *Kaput*. Off the job. I don't know if the King and Queen will forgive you, but if they've got any sense, they won't. You're failures. You're feeble. Pathetic. A disaster. Rescuing a kitchen boy and leaving the Prince!"

Still the rescuers said nothing. They were guilty of everything the harpy accused them of. For they *had* put Ben before the Prince. Hans had struggled with himself for a few minutes, but in the end he and the troll had run back to help Ben and left the true Prince of the Island in a squelchy heap inside the cake. They had forgotten him, it was as simple as that. And Raymond had come to himself and climbed out and even now was probably guzzling Knickerbocker Glories in his room in the hotel. What's more, they hadn't even thought of going back and having another go at getting him out; all they'd thought of was carrying Ben away to safety. They weren't fit to be rescuers; the harpy was right.

"The ghosts told me what happened," said Mrs. Smith. "And if I were the King and Queen, I'd know what to do with you. All that fuss about a common servant boy!"

"He's not a common servant boy, he's *Ben*," raged Odge—and took a step backward as the harpy lifted her dreadful claw and sharpened it once, twice, three times against the step.

"Well, the most useful thing you can do now is keep out of our way," Mrs. Smith went on. "Get yourself through the gump and let us finish the job."

Gurkie put her hand to her heart. She didn't care for Raymond, but the idea of him being carried away in the talons of Mrs. Smith was too horrible to bear.

"How will you operate?" asked the wizard.

"That's none of your business. But some of my girls are sussing out the Astor now. There seems to be a helicopter pad."

She said no more, but in the distance they could hear the baying of a hellhound and a high, screeching voice ordering him to: "*Sit!*"

The harpy flew off then, but the evil she had left in the air still lingered. Then from behind them came a strong young voice.

"Goodness!" said Ben, sitting up and rubbing his head. "What an absolutely *horrible* smell!"

CHAPTER 18

ND, PLEASE, let us get this clear," said Mrs.
Smith. "It is I who will actually snatch the boy. You will
help me, of course; you will take care of his mother and
the guards, but the Prince is *mine*!"

"Yes, Mrs. Smith," said the other harpies gloomily.
"We understand."

They sat in a circle round their chief in a disused
underpass not far from the Astor. No one went there
after dark; it was the sort of place which muggers loved

and ordinary people avoided. All of them would have liked to be the one to snatch the Prince, but they hadn't really expected to be chosen—their leader always kept the best jobs for herself.

Miss Brown, Miss Green, Miss Jones, and Miss Witherspoon were a little smaller than Mrs. Smith, but they had the same rank black wings, the same evil talons, the same stretch tops and bloomers ending in the same frills. They too had handbags full of makeup, but Miss Witherspoon kept a whistle and some dog biscuits in hers. She was the sporting one, the one who trained the dogs.

"You have the sack, Lydia?" asked Mrs. Smith—and Miss Brown nodded.

"And you have the string, Beryl?" she went on—and Miss Green held up the ball of twine.

"Good. We'll parcel him up in the cloakroom—I don't fancy any wriggling as we go through the tunnel." She turned to Miss Witherspoon: "As for the dogs, they'd best stay on the lead till the last moment. I'll give the signal when you should let them go."

One of the black yelpers stirred and got to his feet.

"Sit!" screeched Miss Witherspoon—and the dog sat.

"Now *grovel!*" she yelled—and the great saucer-eyed beast flopped onto his stomach and crawled toward her like a worm.

"Well, that settles everything, I think," said Mrs. Smith. "Just time for a little sleep." She opened her handbag and took out a packet of curlers which she wound into her brassy hair. Then she tucked her head into her wings, as birds do, and in a moment the others heard her snores.

There were only a few more hours before the closing of the gump for nine long years, but it was clear that Mrs. Smith didn't even think of failure. Much as they had wanted to snatch the Prince themselves, the other harpies had to admit that she was the best person for the job.

On the roof of the Astor, Mrs. Trottle waited with her husband and her son. Her suitcase, ready packed, was beside her, and a traveling rug. In ten minutes the helicopter would be there to take them to safety. Mr. Trottle's uncle, Sir Ian Trottle, who lived in a big house on the Scottish border, had offered to shelter them from the madmen who were chasing Raymond.

Her darling babykin hadn't realized that the gang of dope fiends were after him again. When he came round inside the cake, he couldn't remember anything, and she hadn't told him what had happened. And actually she herself wasn't too clear about what had gone on in the Astor dining room. Bruce had told her that he'd thrown the boy for safety into the cake to save him from the clutches of the kidnappers, and she'd rewarded him, but he wasn't much good anymore, limping about and with a bruise on his head the size of a house. And Doreen, who'd been thrown through a window, had cut her wrist so badly that it would be a long time before she could knit. She'd sent them both home, and it was two of the Astor's own guards who were protecting them until the helicopter came.

As for the rest of the babble—something about some boy being lifted up and taken to heaven—Mrs. Trottle put that down to the effect of the poisonous gas that had been let off in the room. By the time she'd got back after some idiot kept her talking on the phone, the dining room was in a shambles and what everyone said was double-dutch.

"I'm hungry!" said Raymond.

"We'll have some sandwiches in the helicopter, dear," said Mrs. Trottle.

"I don't want them in the helicopter, I want them *now*," whined Raymond. He began to grope in Mrs. Trottle's hold-all, found a bar of toffee, and put it in his mouth.

Mrs. Trottle looked up, but there was no sign yet of the helicopter. It was a beautiful clear night. They'd have an easy flight. And as soon as Raymond was safe at Dunloon, she was going to call the police. Once Ben was out of her way and there was no snooping to be done, she'd get proper protection for her little one. And Ben *would* be out of the way—she'd left clear instructions at the hospital. Even now he might be on the way to Ramsden Hall. She'd had a scare with Ramsden— some meddling do-gooders had tried to get the place shut down, but the man who ran it had been too clever for them. Whatever it was called, Ramsden was a good old-fashioned reform school. They didn't actually send children up chimneys because most people now had central heating, but they saw to it that the boys knew their place, and that was what Ben needed. And oh, the relief she'd feel at having him out of the house!

"Here it comes!" said Mr. Trottle, and the guards moved aside the cones and turned up the landing lights, ready for the helicopter to land.

The pilot who'd been sent to fetch the Trottles was one of the best. He had flown in the Gulf War; he was steady and experienced, and of course he would never have taken even the smallest sip to drink before a flight.

And yet now he was seeing things. He was seeing dogs. Which meant that he was going mad because you did not see dogs in the sky; you didn't see stars blotted out by thrashing tails; you didn't see grinning jowls and fangs staring in at the cockpit.

The pilot shook his head. He closed his eyes for an instant, but it didn't help. Another slobbering face with bared teeth and saucer eyes had appeared beside him. There were more of them now . . . three . . . four . . . five.

There couldn't be five dogs racing through the sky. But there were—and they were coming closer. He dipped suddenly, expecting them to be sliced by his propellers, but they weren't. Of course they weren't, because they didn't exist.

High above him, Miss Witherspoon, her handbag dangling, encouraged the pack.

"Go on! See him off!" she shouted. "Faster! Faster!"

Excited by the chase, the dogs moved in. Sparks came from their eyes, spittle dropped from their jaws. The pack leader threw himself at the cockpit window.

The pilot could see the roofs of the Astor below, but every time he tried to lose height, the phantom dogs chivied him harder—and what if those sparks were real? What if they burnt the plane?

"Tally ho!" cried Miss Witherspoon, high in the sky. She blew her whistle, and the dogs went mad.

The pilot made one more attempt to land. Then suddenly he'd had enough. The Astor could wait, and so could the people who had hired him. The Trottles, staring at the helicopter's light as it came down, saw it rise again and vanish over the rooftops.

"Now what?" said Mrs. Trottle, peevishly.

She was soon to find out.

The people of London had forgotten the old ways. They had heard the baying of the phantom yelpers in the sky, and now they could smell the evil stench that came in with the night air, but they spoke of drains, of blocked pipes, and shut their windows.

And the harpies flew on.

"Yuk!" said Raymond, chewing his toffee bar. "It stinks. I feel sick!"

"Well, my little noodle-pie, I did tell you not to eat sweets before—"

Then she broke off, and all the Trottles stared upward.

"My God!" Mr. Trottle staggered backward. "What are they? Ostriches . . . vultures?"

The gigantic birds were losing height. They could see the talons of the biggest one now, caught in the landing lights.

And they could see other things.

"B . . . Bloomers," babbled Mrs. Trottle. "F . . . frills."

"Shoot, can't you!" yelled Mr. Trottle at the guard. "What are we paying you for?"

The guard lifted his gun. There was a loud report, and Mrs. Smith shook out her feathers and smiled. The wings of harpies have been arrow-proof and bullet-proof since the beginning of time.

"Ready, girls!" she called.

The second guard lifted his gun . . . then dropped it and ran screaming back into the building. He had seen a handbag and could take no more.

And the harpies descended.

Each of them knew what to do. Miss Brown landed

on Mrs. Trottle, who had fainted clean away, and sat on her chest. Miss Green picked up the remaining guard and threw him onto the fire escape. Miss Jones pinned the gibbering Mr. Trottle against a wall.

Only Raymond still stood there, his jaws clamped so hard on his treacle toffee that he couldn't even scream.

And then he stood there no longer.

CHAPTER 19

BY THE EVENING of the ninth day, the rescuers could put off their return no longer, but as they made their way to King's Cross Station they felt sadder than they had ever felt in their lives. To come back in disgrace like this . . . to know that they had failed!

Odge, trudging along with the mistmaker's suitcase, was silent and pale, and this worried the others. They had expected her to rant and rave and stamp her feet when Ben once more refused to come with them, but she had behaved well and that wasn't like her. If Odge was going to be ill, that would really be the end.

They had waited till the last minute to make sure Ben had completely recovered from the blow to his head. He'd kept telling them he was fine; he'd helped them to clear up the summer house, sweeping and tidying with a will, and that had made the parting worse because they'd remembered the moment when they first saw him in the basement of Trottle Towers. How happy they'd been when they thought he was the Prince! How certain that they could bring him back!

But there'd been no changing Ben's mind; he wouldn't leave his grandmother. "She's having an operation," he'd said. "I can't leave her to face that alone. Maybe I can come down next time, when the gump opens again."

He'd turned away then, and they knew how much he minded—but Odge hadn't lost her temper the way she'd done before; she'd just shrugged and said nothing at all.

The ghosts were waiting on Platform Thirteen. They looked thoroughly shaken though it was hours since the harpies had come through on their way to rescuing Raymond.

"I tell you, it was like the armies of the dead," said Ernie. "I wouldn't be Raymond Trottle for all the rice in China. They've had engineers here all afternoon looking for blocked drains."

And indeed the harpies' vile stench still lingered. Even the spiders on the stopped clock looked stunned.

Now it was time to say good-bye, and that was hard. The ghosts and the rescuers had become very fond of each other in the nine days they had worked together, but when Cor asked them if they wouldn't come through the gump, they shook their heads.

"Ghosts is ghosts and Islanders is Islanders," said Ernie. "And what would happen to the gump if we weren't here to guard it?"

But the ogre was looking anxiously at the station roof.

"I think we go now?" he said. "I wish not to be under the smelling ladies when they return."

No one wanted that. No one, for that matter, wanted to see the Prince brought back in the harpies' claws like a dead mouse.

They went through into the cloakroom and shook hands. Even the ghost of the train spotter was upset to see them go.

"Please could you take the mistmaker's suitcase for me," said Odge suddenly. "My arm's getting tired."

Gurkie nodded and Odge went forward to the Opening. "I'll go ahead," she said. "I'm missing my sisters and I want to get there quickly."

It says a lot about how weary and sad the rescuers were that they believed her.

. . .

When he came into the ward, Ben saw that the curtains were drawn round Nanny's bed.

"Has she had the operation?" he asked the nurse. It was Celeste, the one with the red rose in her cap whom everyone loved.

"No, dear. She's not going to have the operation. She's—very ill, Ben. You can sit with her quietly—she'd like to have you there, but she may not say much."

Ben drew aside the curtain. He could see at once that something had happened to Nanny. Her face was tiny; she looked as though she didn't really belong here anymore. But when he pulled a chair up beside the bed and reached for her hand, the skinny, brown-flecked fingers closed tightly round his own.

"Foiled 'em!" said Nanny in a surprisingly clear voice.

"About the operation, do you mean?"

"That's right. Going up there full of tubes! Told them my time was up!"

Her eyes shut . . . then fluttered open once again.

"The letter . . . take it . . ." she whispered. "Go on. Now."

Ben turned his head and saw a white envelope with his name on it lying on her locker.

"All right, Nanny." She watched him, never taking her eyes away, as he took it and put it carefully in his pocket. And now she could let go.

"You're a good boy . . . We shouldn't have . . ."

Her voice drifted away; her breathing became shallow and uneven; only her hand still held tightly onto Ben's.

"Just sleep, Nanny," he said. "I'll stay."

And he did, as the clock ticked away the hours. That was what he had to do now, sit beside her, not thinking of anything else. Not letting his mind follow Odge and the others as they made their way home . . . Not feeling sorry for himself because the people he loved so much had gone away. Just being there while Nanny needed him, that was his job.

The night nurse, coming in twice, found him still as stone beside the bed. The third time she came in, he had fallen asleep in his chair—but he still held his grandmother's cold hand inside his own.

Gently, she uncurled his fingers and told him what had happened.

It was hard to understand that he was now absolutely alone. People dying, however much you expect it, is not like you think it will be.

The Sister had taken him to her room; she'd given him tea and biscuits. Now, to his surprise, she said: "I've been in touch with the people who are going to fetch you, and they're on their way. Soon you'll be in your new home."

Ben lifted his head. "What?" he said stupidly.

"Mrs. Trottle has made the arrangements for you, Ben. She's found a really nice place for you, she says. A school where you'll learn all sorts of things. She didn't think you'd want to go on living with the other servants now your grandmother is dead."

Ben was incredibly tired; it was difficult to take anything in. "I don't know anything about this," he said.

The Sister patted his shoulder. Mrs. Trottle had sounded so kind and concerned on the telephone that it never occurred to her to be suspicious.

"Ah, here they are now," she said.

Two men came into the room. They wore natty suits —one pin-striped, one pale gray—and kipper ties. One of them had long dark hair parted in the middle and trained over his ears; the other was fair, with thick curls. Both of them smelled strongly of aftershave, but their fingernails were dirty.

Ben disliked them at once. They looked oily and untrustworthy, and he took a step backward.

"I don't want to go with you," he said. "I want to find out what all this is about."

"Now come on, we don't want a fuss," said the dark-haired man. "My name's Stanford, by the way, and this here is Ralph—and we've got a long drive ahead of us, so let's be off sharpish."

"Where to? Where are we going?"

"The name wouldn't mean anything to you," said

Ralph, putting a comb through his curls. "But you'll be all right there, you'll see. Now say good-bye to the Sister, and we'll be on our way."

The Sister looked troubled. The men were not what she had expected, but her orders were clear. Ben must not leave the hospital alone and in a state of shock.

"I'm sure everything will be all right, dear," she said. "And of course you'll come back for your Granny's funeral."

The men caught each other's eye, and Ralph gave a snigger. One thing the children at Ramsden Hall did *not* get was time off to go to funerals!

Ben was so tired now that nothing seemed real to him. If the Sister thought it was all right, then perhaps it was. And after all, what was there for him now in Trottle Towers?

He picked up his jacket. The letter was still in his pocket, but he didn't want to read it in front of these unpleasant men.

"All right," he said wearily. "I'm ready."

And then, sandwiched between the two thugs Mrs. Trottle had hired to deliver him to as horrible a place as could be found in England, he walked down the long hospital corridor toward the entrance hall.

It was very late. As she trudged through the streets, Odge was dazzled by the headlights of cars and the silly advertisements flashing on and off. Advertisements for stomach pills, for hairspray, for every sort of rubbish. For a moment she wondered if she was going to be able to stand it. On the Island now it would be cool and quiet; the mistmakers would be lying close together on the beaches, and the stars would be bright and clear. It wasn't a very nice thought that she would never see the Island under the stars again. Well, not for nine years. But in nine years she might be as silly as her sisters, talking about men and marriage and all that stuff.

She stopped for a moment under a lamp to look at the map. First right, first left, over a main road and she'd be there.

London wasn't very beautiful, but there were good things here, and good people. The Plodger was kind, and Henry Prendergast, and even quite ordinary people: shop assistants and park keepers. It wouldn't be too bad living here. And she wouldn't miss her bossy sisters—well, perhaps Fredegonda a little. Fredegonda could be quite funny when she was practicing squeezing people's stomachs to give them nightmares.

The mistmaker she'd miss horribly, that was true, but she couldn't have kept him. The way those idiots had carried on in the Astor had shown her that, and he was old enough now to fend for himself. When the others realized that she hadn't gone ahead—that she'd doubled back and hidden in the cloakroom—they'd see to him, and explain to her parents. And even if she wanted to change her mind, it was too late. In an hour from now, the gump would be closed.

"I am a hag," she reminded herself, because rather a bad attack of homesickness was coming on. "I am Odge-with-the-Tooth."

She turned left . . . crossed the road. She could see the hospital now, towering over the other buildings. Ben would be in there still, and when she imagined him watching by the old woman's bed, Odge knew she'd done the right thing. Ben was clever, but he was much too trusting; he needed someone who saw things as they really were. No one was going to get the better of Ben while she was around, and if it meant living in dirty London instead of the Island, well, that was part of the job.

Up the steps of the hospital now. Even so late at night there were lights burning in the big entrance hall. Hospitals never slept.

"I am Miss Gribble," she said, and the reception clerk looked down in surprise at the small figure, dressed in an old-fashioned blazer, which had come in out of the dark. "And I have to see—"

She broke off because someone had called her name —and spinning round, she saw Ben coming toward her, hemmed in by two men. His face was white, he looked completely exhausted, and the men seemed to be helping him.

"Odge!" he called again. "What are you doing here? Why aren't you—"

The man on Ben's right jerked his arm. "Now then— we've no time to chat."

He began to pull Ben toward the door, but Ben twisted round, trying to free himself.

"She's dead, Odge!" he cried. "My grandmother. She's dead!" His voice broke; it was the first time he'd said that word.

Odge drew in her breath. Then she looked at the big clock on the wall. A quarter past eleven. They could do it if they hurried. Just.

"Then you can come with me!" she said joyfully. "You can come back to the Island."

Ben blinked, shook himself properly awake. He had lost all sense of time, sitting by his grandmother's bed; he'd thought it was long past midnight and the gump was closed. Hope sprang into his eyes.

"Let me *go*!" he said, and with sudden strength he

pulled away from his guard. "I'm going with her!"

"Oh no, you aren't!" Stanford grabbed his shoulders; Ralph bent Ben's arm behind his back and held it there. "You're coming with us and pronto. Now walk."

Ben fought as hard as he knew how, but the men were strong and there were two of them. And the receptionist had gone into her office. There was no one to see what was happening and help. They were close to the door now, and the waiting car.

But Odge had dodged round in front of them.

"No, Ben, no! You mustn't hurt the poor men," she said. "Can't you see how ill they are?"

"Get out of the way, you ugly little brat, or we'll take you, too," said Stanford, and kicked out at her.

But Odge still stood there, looking very upset.

"Oh, how dreadful! Your poor hair! I'm so *sorry* for you!"

Without thinking, Stanford put his hand to his head. Then he gave a shriek. A lump of black hair the size of a fist had come out of his scalp.

"That's how it starts," said Odge. "With sudden baldness. The frothing and the fits come later."

"My God!" Stanford grabbed at his temples, and another long, greasy wedge of hair fell onto the lapel of his suit.

"And your friend—he's even worse," said Odge. "All those lovely curls!"

It was true. Ralph's curls were dropping onto the

tiled floor like hunks of knitting wool while round patches of pink skin appeared on his scalp.

"Usually there's no cure," Odge went on, "but maybe they could give you an injection in here. Some hospitals do have a vaccine—it gets injected into your behind with a big needle—but you'd have to hurry!"

The thugs waited no longer. Holding onto their heads, trying uselessly to keep in the rest of their hair, they ran down the corridor shrieking for help.

"Oh Odge!" said Ben. "*You* did it! You struck them with baldness!"

"Don't waste time," said the hag.

She put her hand into Ben's, and together they bounded down the steps and out into the night.

CHAPTER 20

HE THREE-MASTED SCHOONER was at anchor off the Secret Cove. Beside it lay the Royal Yacht with its flying standard, and the charter boat. A number of smaller craft—dinghies and rowing boats—were drawn up on the beach. The tide was out; the clean firm sand curved and rippled round the bay. In the light of the setting sun, the sea was calm and quiet.

But the King and Queen stood with their backs to the sea, facing the round dark hole at the bottom of the cliff. The cave which led to the gump was surrounded by thorn bushes and overhung by a ledge of rock. It was from there that the Prince would come.

If he came at all . . .

Flanking the King and Queen were the courtiers and the important people on the Island. The head teacher of the school had come on the charter boat and the Prime Minister and a little girl who had been top in Latin and won the trip as a prize.

And standing behind the King and Queen, but a little way off because they still hadn't allowed themselves to wash, were Lily and Violet and Rose. Each of them held a firm, unopened banana in her hand, and their eyes too were fixed on the cave.

There were just two hours still to go before the Closing.

"Your Majesty should rest," said the royal doctor, coming forward with a folding stool. "At least sit down; you're using up all your strength."

But the Queen couldn't sit; she couldn't eat or drink; she could only stare at the dark hole in the cliff as if to take her eyes from it would be to abandon the last shred of hope.

At ten-thirty the flares were lit. Flares round the opening, flares along the curving bay now crowded with people. . . . A ring of flares where the King and Queen waited. It was beautiful, the flickering firelight, but frightening too, for it marked the ending of the last day.

But not surely the end of hope?

Five minutes passed . . . ten . . . Then from the crowd lining the shore there came a rustle of excitement . . . a murmuring—and from the Queen a sudden cry.

A lone figure had appeared in the opening. The King and Queen had already moved toward it, when they checked. It was not their son who stood in the mouth of the cave—it was not anyone they knew. It was in fact a very tired witch called Mrs. Harbottle, holding a carrier bag and looking bewildered. She'd heard about the gump from a sorcerer who worked in the Job Center and decided she fancied it.

The disappointment was bitter. The Queen did not weep, but those who stood close to her could see, suddenly, how she would look when she was old.

Another silence—more ticking away of the minutes. A cold breeze blew in from the sea. Rose and Lily and Violet still held their closed bananas, but Lily had begun to snivel.

Then once more the mouth of the cave filled with figures. Well-known ones this time—and once more hope leapt up, only to die again. There was no need to ask if the rescuers had, after all, brought back the Prince. Cor was bent and huddled into his cloak; Gurkie carried her straw basket as if the weight was too much to bear—and where the fernseed had worn off, they could see the ogre's red, unhappy face.

From just a few people on the shore there came

hisses and boos, but the others quickly shushed them. They knew how terrible the rescuers must feel, coming back empty-handed, and that failure was punishment enough.

Cor was too ashamed to go and greet the King and Queen. He moved out of the light of the flares and sat down wearily on a rock. Gurkie was looking for Odge in the crowd gathered on the beach. She could make out two of Odge's sisters, but there was no sign of the little hag—and trying not to think what a homecoming this might have been, she went to join Cor and the ogre in the shadows.

"We must go and speak to them," said the King. "They will have done their best."

"Yes." But before the Queen could gather up her strength, the child who had won the Latin prize put up her hand.

"Listen!" she said.

Then the others heard it too. Baying. Barking. Howling. The sky yelpers were back!

They burst out of the opening—the whole pack—tumbling over each other, slobbering, slavering, their saucer eyes glinting. Freed suddenly from the tunnel, they hurled themselves about, sending up sprays of loose sand.

But not for long! The smell came first—and then Miss Witherspoon, holding her whistle.

"Sit!" screamed the harpy—and the dogs sat.

"Grovel!" she screeched, and the dogs flopped onto their stomachs, slobbering with humbleness.

"Stay!" she yelled—and they stayed.

Then she stepped aside. The smell grew worse, and out of the tunnel, feet first, came Miss Green, Miss Brown, and Miss Jones. The monstrous bird-women's wings were furled, and one look at their smug faces showed the watchers what they wanted to know.

Turning, the harpies took their place on either side of the tunnel and stretched out their arms with their dangling handbags. "Lo!" they seemed to be saying as they pointed to the opening. "Behold! The Great One comes!"

A cheer went up then and to the sound of hurrahs and the sight of waving hands, Mrs. Smith appeared in the mouth of the cave.

And in her arms—a sack! A large sack, tied at the top but heaving and bulging so that they knew what was inside it was very much alive.

The Prince! The Prince had come!

All eyes went to the King and Queen. The Queen stood with her hand to her heart. He had come in a sack, as a prisoner—but he had come! Nothing mattered except that.

But before she could move forward, the chief harpy put up her arm. She had decided to drop Raymond at the feet of the King and Queen—to sail through the air with him, like the giant birds in the stories. Now she

picked up the sack in her talons; unfurled her wings—
and circling the heads of the crowd, holding the squirm-
ing bundle in her iron claws, she came down and, with
perfect timing, dropped it on a hummock of sand.

"I bring you His Royal Highness, the Prince of the
Island," said Mrs. Smith—and patted her perm.

The cheering had stopped. No one stirred now, no one
spoke. This was the moment they had waited for for
nine long years.

The harpy bent down to the sack—and the King ban-
ished her with a frown. Later she would be rewarded, but
no stranger was going to unwrap this precious burden.

"Your scissors," he said to the doctor.

The doctor opened his black bag and handed them
over. The Queen was deathly pale; her breath came in
gasps as she stood beside her husband.

With a single snip, the King cut the string, unwound
it, loosened the top of the sack. The Queen helped him
ease it over the boy's shoulders. Then with a sudden
slurp like a grub coming out of an egg, the wriggling
figure of Raymond Trottle fell out on the sand.

He wasn't just wriggling; he was yelling, he was
howling, he was kicking. Snot ran from his nose as he
tried to fight off the Queen's gentle hands.

"I want my Mummy! I want my Mummy! I want to
go home!" sobbed Raymond Trottle.

The nurses stepped forward, their unzipped bananas in their hands—and stepped back, zipping them up again. And a great worry fell over the watchers on the shore because even from a distance they could see the Prince kicking out at his parents and hear his screams, and now as the King set him firmly on his feet, they saw his piggy, swollen face and the hiccuping sobs that came from him. Would the Queen not be terribly hurt at the way her son was carrying on?

They needn't have worried. The Queen had straightened herself; and as she lifted her face, they saw that she was looking most wonderfully and radiantly happy. The years fell away from her, and she might have been a girl of seventeen. Then the King followed her gaze, and the watching crowd saw this brave man become transfigured too and change into the carefree ruler they had known.

On the ground, the boy the harpies had brought continued to kick and scream, and the Queen very politely moved her skirt away from him, but she did not run. She moved the way people do in dreams, half gliding, half dancing, as though there was all the time and happiness in the wide world—and the King moved with her, his hand under her arm.

Only then did the onlookers turn their heads to the mouth of the cave and see two figures standing there. One was the little hag, Odge Gribble. The other was a boy.

A boy who for an instant stood quite still with a look of wonder on his face. Then he let go of Odge's hand, and he *did* run. He ran like the wind, scarcely touching the ground—nor did he stop when he reached the King and Queen, but threw himself into their arms as though all his life had led to this moment.

And now the three figures became one, and as the King and Queen held him and encircled him, the watchers heard the same words repeated again and again.

"My son! My son! My *son*!"

CHAPTER 21

ODGE GRIBBLE had moved into the nurses' cave. A week had passed since Ben had gone to the palace to live, and she hadn't heard a single word from him. Now she was going to retire from the world and become a hermit. She had left a note for her mother and her sisters, and she was settling in.

The nurses had eaten burnt toast and slept on stones and poked sticks into their ears, but the things Odge was going to do were much more interesting than that.

She was going to sleep on rusty spikes and eat slime and raw jellyfish. She wasn't going to talk to a living soul ever again, and every day and in every way she was going to get more awful and fearful and hag-like. By the time she was grown up, she would be known as Odge of the Cave, or Odge of the Ocean, or just Odge the Unutterable. The cave would be full of frogs she had coughed; *all* her teeth would be blue, and the bump on her left foot would have turned not into one extra toe, but into seven of them at least.

Now she unpacked her suitcase. It was the one the mistmaker had traveled in, but of course Ben had taken the mistmaker with him to the palace. It was her pet really, but Ben hadn't cared; he'd just gone off with his parents to be a prince and never given her another thought. They said that when people became grand and famous, they forgot their friends, and Ben certainly proved it.

She found a flat boulder which would do as a table and decided to have moldy bladder wrack for lunch. She wouldn't eat with a knife and fork either; she'd eat with her fingers so as to become disgusting as quickly as possible. Now that the nurses did nothing but guzzle beautiful bananas and parade around in frilled dresses which they washed three times a day, it was time some-one remembered sorrow and awfulness.

She found the bladder wrack all right; it even had

some little worms crawling on it, but she decided to have lunch a bit later. Not that she was going to be beaten; she'd eat it in the end, all of it. She wasn't going to be beaten by *anything*. No one was going to hurt her again, and she wasn't going back to school either. She had enjoyed school, but she wasn't going to enjoy anything anymore *ever*, and that would show them!

But as she sat with her toes in an icy pool, waiting for them to turn blue and perhaps even drop off with frostbite, she couldn't help thinking how cruel and unfair life was. For it was she who had brought Ben through the gump, and if she hadn't made him open his grandmother's letter as the taxi took them to King's Cross, he might still have argued about coming and perhaps not being welcome on the Island.

Odge could remember every word that Nanny Brown had written.

"Dear Ben," the letter began. "I have to tell you that something very bad was done to you when you were little. You see, you were kidnapped by Mrs. Trottle. She snatched you from your basket near King's Cross Station and carried you off to Switzerland, meaning to pass you off as her own child. But when she got there, she found she was expecting a baby of her own, and after Raymond was born to her, she turned against you and would have sent you away, only I wouldn't let her. No one knows who your real parents are, but they must have loved you very much because you were wearing the most beautiful clothes and the comforter in your mouth was on a golden ring.

"So you must go the police at *once*, Ben, and tell them the truth and ask them to help you find your family—and please forgive me for the lies I told you all those years."

The whole thing had made sense to Odge at once. Ben must have been so much nicer to look at than Raymond, and cleverer, and better able to do things. No wonder Mrs. Trottle had got annoyed and tried to send him away.

And Ben *was* nice—he was as nice as Raymond was nasty—so that it hurt all the more that he had forgotten her. True, the King and Queen had hugged her and the other rescuers and said how grateful they were—and it was true too that the short time between Ben coming through and the Closing had been incredibly busy. Raymond had had to be packed up and thrown into one of the last of the wind baskets that went up to King's Cross, and what the ghosts of the gump thought when they saw him was anybody's guess. And just as Raymond went up, there was a great surge of last-minute people coming down: the Plodger with a bundle of wet cloths which turned out to be his niece Melisande, and the troll called Henry Prendergast, and two of the banshees who'd got wind of the fact that Raymond wasn't the Prince and decided to come to the Island after all.

Even so, Odge had at first not believed that she was forgotten. Every day she had waited at least to be asked to tea at the palace, or thought Ben might ride by her home and ask how she was. Everyone told stories about him—about his white pony, his intelligence, the great wolfhound his father had given him, and the happiness of the Queen who looked so beautiful that the King had had to post a special guard at the palace gates to take in the bunches of flowers which besotted young men left for her.

Well, that's nothing to do with me, thought Odge. I shall stay here in the darkness and the cold and get shriveled and old, and one day they'll find a heap of bones in the corner—and then they'll be sorry.

She was sitting in the mouth of the cave, her hands round her knees, and coughing, when she saw a boy picking his way between the mistmakers on the sands. As he came closer she saw who it was, but she didn't take any notice, she just went on coughing.

"Hello!" said Ben. He looked incredibly well and incredibly happy. She'd have liked to see him wearing silly clothes to show he was royal, but he wasn't—he wore a blue shirt and cotton trousers, and he'd come alone.

"What are you doing?" asked Ben, surprised.

"I'm trying to cough frogs, if you really want to

know," said Odge. "Not that it's any business of yours."

Ben looked round to see if there were any frogs there, but there weren't.

"Odge, I don't know why you're so keen on coughing them. What would you do with them if you did cough them? Ten to one, they'd start thinking they were enchanted princes and wanting you to kiss them and what then?"

Odge sniffed. "I haven't the slightest idea why you've come," she said. "As you see, I've moved in here and I'm going to live here for the rest of my life."

"Why?" asked Ben, sitting down beside her.

Odge drew her hair round her face and disappeared. "Because I want to be alone. I don't want to live in the world, which is full of ingratitude and pain. And I can't help wondering what you're doing sitting on the ground? Why didn't you bring your throne, an important prince like you?"

Ben looked at her amazed. "What on earth's got into you?" he asked.

"Nothing. I told you, I'm going to live here for the rest of my life."

But Ben had seen, in a chink between her hair, the glint of tears. "I see. Well, that's rather a waste because we've spent a whole week decorating your room and furnishing it so as to be a surprise. I suppose I shall just have to tell my parents that you don't want to come, but they'll be terribly disappointed."

"What room?" asked Odge faintly.

"Your room; I've told you. The one next to mine in the palace. It was painted pink, and we didn't think that was right for a hag, so my mother chose a midnight-blue wallpaper with a frieze of bats, and she put a cat door in for the mistmaker, and you've got a huge bed stuffed with raven's feathers—the ravens *gave* their feathers because you're a heroine. It's pretty nice. And my mother drove over to your mother this morning to ask if you could come and live, and your mother said it was all right as long as you visit once a week. So it's kind of a pity about the cave."

He waited. Odge turned her head. Her green eye appeared; then her brown one as she shook back her hair.

"Really? You want me to live with you?"

"Of course. We decided it on the first day, my parents and I," said Ben, and when he said "my parents" his whole face seemed to light up. "Perhaps we should have told you, only I love surprises and I thought maybe you do too."

"Well, yes, I do actually." She scuffed her shoes on the sand. "Only . . . what if I don't turn out to be . . . you know . . . mighty and fearful? Would they want to have a hag that's just . . . ordinary . . . living in a palace? I mean, I may *never* get an extra toe."

Ben got to his feet. "Don't be silly, Odge," he said. You're *you* and it's you we want."

Odge blew her nose and put her pajamas back in the suitcase. Then she gave Ben her hand, and together they walked along the shore toward the welcoming roofs of the palace.

Eva Ibbotson has written several books for children and adults. A previous novel, *Which Witch?*, was a runner-up for the Carnegie Medal, one of England's most prestigious children's book prizes. Ms. Ibbotson lives in the north of England.

Sue Porter has illustrated more than fifty books for children. She lives with her husband and their three children in the countryside of Rutland, England.